THE
CATERPILLAR DOGS
AND
OTHER EARLY
STORIES

BY TENNESSEE WILLIAMS

PLAYS

Camino Real (with *Ten Blocks on the Camino Real*)

Candles to the Sun

Cat on a Hot Tin Roof

Clothes for a Summer Hotel

Fugitive Kind

The Glass Menagerie

A House Not Meant to Stand

A Lovely Sunday for Creve Coeur

The Night of the Iguana

Not About Nightingales

The Notebook of Trigorin

Orpheus Descending & Suddenly Last Summer

The Rose Tattoo (with *The Dog Enchanted by the Divine View*)

Something Cloudy, Something Clear

Spring Storm

Stairs to the Roof

A Streetcar Named Desire

Sweet Bird of Youth (with *The Enemy: Time*)

Baby Doll & Tiger Tail

The Two-Character Play

Vieux Carré

THE THEATRE OF TENNESSEE WILLIAMS

The Theatre of Tennessee Williams, Volume I

Battle of Angels, A Streetcar Named Desire, The Glass Menagerie

The Theatre of Tennessee Williams, Volume II

The Eccentricities of a Nightingale, Summer and Smoke, The Rose Tattoo, Camino Real

The Theatre of Tennessee Williams, Volume III

Cat on a Hot Tin Roof, Orpheus Descending, Suddenly Last Summer

The Theatre of Tennessee Williams, Volume IV

Sweet Bird of Youth, Period of Adjustment, The Night of the Iguana

The Theatre of Tennessee Williams, Volume V

The Milk Train Doesn't Stop Here Anymore, Kingdom of Earth (The Seven Descents of Myrtle), Small Craft Warnings, The Two-Character Play (Out Cry)

The Theatre of Tennessee Williams, Volume VI

27 Wagons Full of Cotton and Other Short Plays
Includes all the plays from the individual volume of *27 Wagons Full of Cotton and Other Plays* plus *The Unsatisfactory Supper, Steps Must be Gentle, The Demolition Downtown*

The Theatre of Tennessee Williams, Volume VII

In the Bar of a Tokyo Hotel and Other Plays
Includes all the plays from the individual volume of *Dragon Country* plus *Lifeboat Drill, Now the Cats with Jeweled Claws, This is the Peaceable Kingdom*

The Theatre of Tennessee Williams, Volume VIII

Vieux Carré, A Lovely Sunday for Creve Coeur, Clothes for a Summer Hotel, The Red Devil Battery Sign

SCREENPLAYS

Baby Doll & Tiger Tail

Stopped Rocking and Other Screen Plays
All Gaul is Divided, The Loss of a Teardrop Diamond, One Arm, Stopped Rocking

The West End Lyric Theater on Delmar Boulevard in St. Louis
was near the Williams family home and may be the model for
the movie theater in "Every Friday Nite is Kiddies Nite."
Photo by George Dorrill, 1937.

TENNESSEE WILLIAMS

THE
CATERPILLAR DOGS
AND
OTHER EARLY
STORIES

EDITED, WITH AN INTRODUCTION, BY
TOM MITCHELL

A NEW DIRECTIONS BOOK

The Caterpillar Dogs and Other Early Stories is published by special arrangement with The University of the South, Sewanee, Tennessee.

Manufactured in the United States of America
First published as New Directions Paperbook 1556 in 2023

Library of Congress Cataloging-in-Publication Data:
Names: Williams, Tennessee, 1911–1983, author. | Mitchell, Tom (Stage director), editor.
Title: The caterpillar dogs : and other early stories / Tennessee Williams ; edited, with an introduction by Tom Mitchell.
Description: First edition. | New York : New Directions Publishing, 2023.
Identifiers: LCCN 2022050575 | ISBN 9780811232326 (paperback) | ISBN 9780811232333 (ebook)
Subjects: LCGFT: Short stories.
Classification: LCC PS3545.I5365 C38 2023 | DDC 813/.54—dc23/eng/20221020
LC record available at https://lccn.loc.gov/2022050575

10 9 8 7 6 5 4 3 2 1

New Directions Books are published for James Laughlin
by New Directions Publishing Corporation
80 Eighth Avenue, New York 10011

TABLE OF CONTENTS

INTRODUCTION:

EPISODES FROM
THE LIFE OF A CLERK

In 1932, after three years and no degree from the University of Missouri, Thomas Lanier Williams began laboring as an anonymous clerk for the next three years, typing orders, checking inventory, and secretly scribbling poems on shoebox lids in the St. Louis headquarters of the International Shoe Company. Never supportive of his son's academic ambitions, Cornelius Williams finally lost patience with Tom, as he was then known, when he flunked ROTC. He insisted that the young man withdraw from the university to take a job at the shoe company where Cornelius was a sales manager. Leaving college on the verge of his senior year was humiliating; Tom gave up friendships and the first independence he had known, transitioning from the free-wheeling campus atmosphere to a dysfunctional household and a complex, polluted city. Toiling at home in the evenings, Tom composed poems, one-act plays, and short stories that he submitted to magazines and contests. Writing was his means of escape.

The Williams household was filled with turmoil, a family situation that had been rocky since his early childhood. The Williamses had moved from the small Delta town of Clarksdale, Mississippi to St. Louis in 1918, when Tom was seven years old. Though he spent his next school year and many summers with his grandparents in Clarksdale, the family's relocation to St. Louis permanently changed the trajectory of Tom's life. His mother, Edwina, a pampered, sexually repressed minister's daughter prone to hysteria and paranoia, was ill-equipped to cope with raising a family, let alone doing so in the crowded city of St. Louis. Fueled by Cornelius's gambling and heavy drinking, the two fought constantly as they moved the family from one rented flat to another in search of comfort and status. Throughout their school years, Tom and his older sister Rose found themselves outsiders among their classmates in one school after another. Tom grew to rely on his sister for stability, but during their adolescence Rose began to show signs of a mental break, her outbursts and preoccupations eventually becoming more intense and often of a sexual nature.

Rose and Tom were teenagers during the liberated Roaring Twenties, but in their home Edwina would shut-down any mention of sex or intimacy. Nevertheless, when Tom went to college, he provided his sister with tantalizing gossip about fraternity life on campus. Rose, in turn, sent her brother the racy *Ballyhoo* magazine full of naughty comics and suggestive parodies, and referred to herself as "a smoking, dancing, card-playing Sunday School teacher." Despite her expression of boldness, Rose's mental state precluded any serious love affairs, and although he was drawn to the scandalous novels of D.H. Lawrence, Tom's social life in St. Louis was limited, his romantic life was nonexistent, and his sexual orientation unclear.

Outside the Williams home, St. Louis was in the grip of the Great Depression. A riot outside City Hall led to the death of a Black man shot by police while protesting the city government's lack of compassion for the poor. Labor strikes shut down major companies. Unemployed youth hopped aboard freight cars that crisscrossed the city. A "Hooverville" of makeshift shelters stretched along the Mississippi River, where the Gateway Arch now stands. Racial and ethnic neighborhoods shifted as the economy displaced residents. Williams befriended leaders in the Communist Party-allied Union of St. Louis Artists and Writers. Joe Jones, from the organization, taught art classes for unemployed African American men until police locked them out of their studio for creating a mural critical of civic and religious leaders. Another associate of Tom Williams, the author Jack Conroy, published fiery proletarian novels, and local author Josephine Johnson received the Pulitzer Prize for *Now in November,* a novel about the crushing economic burden felt by Missouri farmers. In Tom Williams's neighborhood, radical students from Washington University marched in the streets, and progressive theatre groups produced anti-war and pro-labor plays—he found himself amidst the swirling political and artistic energy of the city, which influenced his early writing.

Tom's workdays were filled typing forms, delivering boxes, and taking orders from impersonal bosses. His days ended writing in isolation, shut away in his small room to spite his father, avoid his mother, and hide from his sister. Already honing his skill as a keen observer of life, he wrote about the characters around him: in poetry and short plays, as well as stories, he imagined their inner lives, ambitions, and deceptions, and in this way, he also began to write about himself. Based on his success as a writer of short fiction in high school when his 1928 story "The Vengeance of Nitocris" was published in *Weird Tales,* he submitted stories to literary magazines identifying himself as an "undiscovered" talent. Following up on awards he'd received in collegiate writing competitions, he submitted work for contests to groups such as the St. Louis Writers' Guild where his stories gained more recognition. He won their first prize for his story "Stella for Star," and in a letter to novelist Josephine Johnson, he wrote, "As you are the only member of the Writers' Guild with whom I have any personal acquaintance, I am addressing this note of thanks to you and hope you will extend it verbally to the rest of the Guild and the contest judges." His letter continued with a self-assessment of his writing. "It is full of bombastic irrelevancies, the characters aren't logically developed, and the romantic spirit . . . is almost unbearably sweet. But I was only trying to create a single, poetic effect and think I may have succeeded a little in doing that."

A month after receiving the St. Louis Writers' Guild award in 1935, Tom Williams had a nervous breakdown, most likely brought on by his soul-crushing job and news of the engagement of his childhood friend, Hazel Kramer, whom he had long dreamed of marrying. To heal from this collapse, Tom was sent to Memphis for the summer with his grandparents, and while there, he began to write plays in earnest. When he returned to St. Louis, Williams joined a dynamic amateur theatre group, The Mummers, and forged a new identity as a playwright. Two years later, he left St. Louis for the playwriting program at the University of Iowa, after which he finally escaped his family and migrated to New Orleans in 1939. He changed his identity from Thomas Lanier Williams to Tennessee Williams. Most of the stories written during his youth in St. Louis were stored away in his mother's basement while the author turned his attention primarily to the theater.

The young Tennessee Williams found escape from his difficult family and meaningless job by writing. His experience of life in an industrial city undergoing dramatic social change permeated his writing in the 1930s. Although Tom Williams never hopped the trains, never took a role in local politics, or marched in the streets, as a young writer he was a romantic proletarian, or as scholar Christopher Bigsby has referred to him, "a radical of the heart." The stories collected here are sketches of fellow citizens. They are "Episodes from the Life of a Clerk," specifically from the life of the anonymous clerk, Tom Williams, working in the International Shoe Company's downtown skyscraper. The characters, like their author, find themselves in a society gripped by economic depression and undergoing enormous social change: a love-sick college student, a retired clergyman, a vacationing stenographer, shotgun-toting lovers, the son of Polish immigrants, ancestor of Spanish conquistadors, and a desperate clerk very much like Williams himself. In each episode, Williams revealed their truth, writing them with empathy, humor, and courage.

Tom Mitchell

THE
CATERPILLAR DOGS
AND
OTHER EARLY
STORIES

THE CATERPILLAR DOGS

In the summer of her eighty-ninth year, Miss Angela De Menjos seemed for the first time rather close to refuting the ancient hypothesis that wealthy spinsters never die. In body she was as perniciously hale as ever. But her terrible old mind showed signs of a rapid deterioration. All of her life she had lived with a frustrated violence. Now a terrible calm was coming upon her. She kept moving constantly around her little flat in the fashionable West End; she nearly worked her middle-aged housekeeper to death by disarranging things as soon as they were put straight. She would yank the covers off of beds, rip curtains from their rods and pictures from the walls, overturn chairs, and scatter silver about the floor. But there was nothing tempestuous in her movements. They were all performed with a deadly, resolute calm. Her tongue, too, was singularly quiet. Sometimes it even seemed that she had lost the faculty of speech. Only her large black eyes still blazed under the huge, bluish-black wig that she wore.

Angela De Menjos was the last of her line. It was a line of Castilian adventurers, conquistadors, and pirates. It is doubtful if, for hundreds of years, any of the De Menjoses had known two consecutive hours of real peace. One branch had sailed with Cortez and settled in Mexico, amassed huge lands, and lived in continual strife with their neighbors. The other branch had taken to buccaneering; sailed on the Spanish Main for several generations; finally settled in Georgia in time for the colonial rebellion. Through a strange series of events the last of the Georgia branch of the De Menjoses, a high-spirited young girl, had met and married the last of the Mexican branch, a fiery young Don. Their only child was Angela, who was unfortunately born a little more woman than man. In her blood was all the fury and courage of the conquistadors, and all the savagery and lawlessness of the buccaneers. But she was born too late for the Spanish Main. There were no more worlds to conquer. She was not even well-fitted for the minor warfare of love. Her nature was too masculine and her body too ugly to appeal to any but the most arrant fortune-hunters, and those she understood and despised. When she was nearly twenty her mother shot her father in a fit of unhappy passion, and then turned the pistol upon herself. From then on, Angela had roamed the world looking for trouble and found practically none. Thirty years ago, she had settled down in Saint Louis. Settled down geographically speaking. Even in this quiet, Middle-Western city she had lived with a frustrated fury. Belatedly passion had come into her life. She fell very much in love with a young coachman whom she employed her first winter in Saint Louis. She remained in the city for three years on his account; he was married and wouldn't leave. After breaking with him in a scene of terrible violence (she hammered him over the head with a whip handle till he was insensible), she continued to live in the city because her wealth and eccentricity had made her a local celebrity, especially around the apartment-hotels among which she rotated. She went in for a long series of gigolo-chauffeurs. Their artificial passion gave her little satisfaction. She employed a different one every two or three months, often breaking into print, and having to pay heavy fines for inflicting violence upon them. At about seventy, sexual passion smoldered out of her nature. Then her life became indeed a torturing frustration. She traveled around a little more, spent two seasons in an Alpine sanitarium, visited many psychiatrists in London, Paris, and Vienna, tried all kinds of cures for all kinds of imaginary ailments. Thinking she had cancer, she returned to Saint Louis to die. But remained there in excellent health for fifteen years more . . . till the summer of her eighty-ninth year, when this terrific, silent calm began to settle over her mind, indicating that the end must be near.

For the last three years, Angela had kept a middle-aged housekeeper to look after her little flat. The woman was a fat widow, invested with such a cowish tranquility that even this ancient daughter of conquistadors and buccaneers could seldom ruffle her spirit. She had one consuming interest and that was dogs. To her distress, Miss De Menjos would not tolerate a dog around the place. She seemed, indeed, to have a special detestation for the animals. As her mistress's mind began to fail, however, the housekeeper conceived a very cunning deceit. She bought a pair of beautiful, fluffy-brown Pekinese and kept them in the cellar of the apartment. When Miss De Menjos heard them barking or saw them scampering about the courtyard of the apartment and enquired furiously whence they had issued, the housekeeper said that they belonged to the young lady across the hall.

For some peculiar reason, all of the old spinster's ebbing fury concentrated itself that summer upon the twin Pekinese. Whenever she heard their small, shrill yapping in the courtyard she would fairly boil. Presumably because of their furry, horizontal appearance, she called them the caterpillar dogs. Leaning out of her window, she would try vainly to shoo them out of the courtyard, waving her stick and hissing, "Scat, scat, you caterpillar dogs! Scat!"

But the dogs were peculiarly unperturbed by her enmity. Once in a while they would lift their black pug faces toward her window and stare coldly up at her with large, shining brown eyes. Then they would wag their fluffy brown plumes and scamper about the yard as peacefully as ever. If they had returned her fury, barking at her or showing any sign of resentment, she would have felt better. Their complete indifference to her existence drove her nearly mad.

Finally she called up the young lady across the hall. She was so agitated that her voice was barely intelligible over the phone. She kept repeating, "I won't have them snuffing about my garden, those nasty caterpillar dogs!"

When eventually the young lady understood what she was talking about and had any chance of reciprocal speech, she angrily disclaimed any connection with the dogs, reminded Angela that the courtyard was not her exclusive property, and finally, and most infuriatingly, expressed a hearty approval of the twin Pekinese.

One Saturday afternoon toward the end of July the occupants of the apartments were treated to an exciting spectacle in the courtyard. While the Pekinese were out for a little air, trotting and snuffing around the flower-bordered court, Miss De Menjos suddenly emerged from her wing of the building, flourishing a long and glittering cutlass. This was a relic that had been handed down to her from the buccaneering branch of the De Menjos family. With this well-preserved weapon, which had been steeped in the blood of countless sailors and sea-captains, red-coats, Mexicans, and Yankees (some De Menjos having wielded it in every American war since the Revolution), the last of the blood-lusting De Menjoses pursued the twin Pekinese round and round the courtyard. No one, not even the housekeeper, who loved the two dogs as her own soul, dared to intervene in this terrible chase. The janitor, who had been watering the lawn, turned his hose full upon Miss De Menjos, thinking that a cold shower might restore her senses. With a piratical yell and flourish of the cutlass, she put him headlong to rout, cutting a gash in the cuff of his pants as he leapt over the hedge. Then she resumed her chase of the dogs. Foolishly, they declined to seek shelter in the building, although the housekeeper held the door open and called them wildly. Indeed, they seemed not to appreciate the seriousness of their situation. Narrowly evading the cutlass time after time, they continued to scamper around Miss De Menjos's maniacal figure. They barked joyously, apparently thinking that this was a little game. Whenever she turned to slash at one of them the other would jump behind her and snap at her skirts. For a woman of eighty-nine years she moved with an amazing energy. But the caterpillar dogs were too much for her. She tired quickly. Her breath came in long, horrible gasps, and her form tottered this way and that. But the cutlass never dropped; it never ceased wildly slashing the air! Her face glistened red with sweat and fury; her great eyes sparkled like black flames. Her wig slipped down on her forehead. Her voice cracked and quivered ecstatically as she shrieked invectives in English and Spanish at the gay Pekinese. For the first time in her life she was fully enjoying herself. The gigolo-chauffeurs had been passive beneath her blows. They had been too terrified to strike back. Here at last was something that would engage with her in physical combat. Here at last was something that snapped at her and barked and flew menacingly around her figure. Here was something of what she had been wanting all her life.

"You caterpillar dogs!" she shrieked. "You dirty little caterpillar dogs! I'll stop you snuffing around my garden! I'll cut your *heads* off! I'll skin you *alive*!"

With a final access of rapturous fury, Miss De Menjos flung her sword through the air at one of the scampering beasts. It landed harmlessly two feet behind his flying brown plume. While it was still hurtling through the air, Miss De Menjos, with a last blood-curdling, piratical yell, had stumbled to the earth. She was dead as a stone before any of the dazed apartment-dwellers could summon courage enough to emerge from the building.

The two caterpillar dogs were the first, in fact, to reach her side.

With long, hot tongues they affectionately licked her dying, red-sweating face, and snapped playfully at her thin, curving brown fingers. One of them seized the great wig like a captured flag, and sailed with it round and round the sunlit yard.

SEASON OF GRAPES

As I was going to enter college that fall, my parents felt that I should build myself up at a summer camp of some sort. They sent me down to a place in the Ozarks on a beautiful lake. It was called a camp but it was not just for boys. It was for both sexes and all ages. It was a rustic, comfortable place. But I was disappointed to find that most of the young people went to another camp several miles down the lake toward the dam. I spent a great deal of time by myself that summer, which is hardly good for a boy of seventeen.

It was a dry summer. There were very few days of rain. But the Ozark country, with its gentle green hills and clear lakes and rivers, did not turn ugly and brown as most countries do in seasons of drought. The willows along the lake remained translucently green, while the hillside forests, toward the end of July, began to look as though they had been splashed with purple, red, and amber wine. Their deepening colors did not suggest dryness, nor stoppage of life. They looked, rather, like a flaming excess, a bursting opulence of life. And the air, when you drove through the country in an open car, was faintly flavored with wine, for the grapes grew plentifully that season. While the cornfields yellowed and languished, the purple grapes fairly swarmed from their vines, as though they had formed some secret treaty with nature or dug into some hidden reservoir of subterranean life, and the lean hill-folk piled them into large white baskets and stood along the sunny roads and highways crying, "*Grapes, grapes, grapes,*" so that your ears, as well as your eyes and nostrils and mouth, were filled with them, until it seemed that the whole body and soul of the country was somehow translated into this vast efflorescence of sweet purple fruit.

Perhaps it was the intoxicating effect of the wine-flavored air, perhaps it was only the novelty of being so much by myself, but I fell that summer into a sort of enchantment, a sort of moody drunkenness, that troubled and frightened me more than a little.

9

I had led an active boy's life. I had always been the typical young extrovert, delighting in games and the companionship of other boys, having little time for reading and abstract thinking, having little time for looking inward upon the mystery of myself, and so this dry summer on the beautiful lake, as I fell slowly into the habit of deep introspection, brooding and dreaming about myself and life and the meaning of things, I felt as though I were waking up from a long dream or sinking into one. I was lonely and frightened and curiously content.

It became my custom that summer to go down to the lake by myself right after breakfast, unmoor a rowboat or a canoe from the rickety grey wharf, and row or paddle out to the center of the lake and then lie down in the boat's bottom, take off all clothes but my swimming trunks, and let the slow current carry me along under the golden-burning sun while my consciousness surrendered itself, like the boat, to a leisurely tide of reveries and dreams.

Sometimes I would fall asleep while I drifted. I would awake to find myself in an unfamiliar country. I had drifted several miles from the camp, perhaps, and the sun had climbed to its zenith while I slept. The lake had narrowed or widened, or perhaps I had drifted in close to shore, and directly beside me was a wet wall of grey rock from which obtruded strange ferns and flowers, or over my head was a fantastic, green-gold, feathery dome of willow branches, overshadowing myself and my stranded vessel with barely a motion, barely a whisper, in the windless noon.

Always beyond me, further down the lake, were the open fields of grapes, and however still the air was, it always held faintly the flavor of wine.

I would lie there in the bottom of the boat and continue to stare at what my eyes had opened upon, never turning my head or moving my body for fear of breaking the spell. I would imagine that I had actually drifted into some unknown place while I slept, some mythical kingdom, an Avalon or something, in which all kinds of things could happen and usually did.

It was hard to shake myself out of these dreams. It was hard to turn my eyes—staring as though hypnotized at the wet wall of grey rock or the dazzling dome of sunlit willows—back to the olive green expanse of the lake. I would feel strangely dull inside and fagged out when I finally roused myself. It was not merely the drowsiness that you feel after a long midday sleep. It was more like the aftereffects of a powerful drug. Sometimes I would feel so weak that it would be hard for me to row or paddle back against the current. Still, I would never know exactly what had gone on inside me during the dream, or how long it had lasted, or why, in heaven's name, I behaved like this! Was I losing my mind?

As summer slipped by, the population of the little camp increased. Each weekend a new crowd or two would drive down from Saint Louis or Kansas City or still further away. When I first arrived, early in June, the place had seemed deserted, and I had felt bitterly lonely and wished that some people, any kind of people, would come. But now I had changed. I no longer felt a thrill of anticipation when a new group or family arrived at the camp, wondering each time how this bunch would turn out, observing with pleasure their equipment for sports, but disappointed, usually, because most of them were either too young or too old. Now the sight of a dust-covered car rolling up the camp drive with tennis racquets and fishing rods, and eager faces protruding from the windows, faces smiling and begging to be accepted into this place and its life, gave me no pleasure, but filled me instead with a vague annoyance. I was becoming like a grumpy old man who wanted nothing so much as a quiet place to sleep, only it was not to sleep that I wanted, but to dream.

Then I began to be really frightened of myself. I quit going out alone on the lake. I made friends with a young professor who was spending his vacation at the camp. I played tennis and learned contract bridge with some young married couples. I tried not to think of the sun on the lake and on my naked skin and the faint, delicious fragrance of the purple grapes.

Toward the end of the summer I met a young girl. I did not think her especially attractive. She did not seem either pretty or homely. Perhaps she was really beautiful, but I was then too young to find beauty in anything but the outlines of a woman's face and figure. She was considerably older than I; she was about twenty-five, and I could see that she was lonely, terribly lonely, and was wanting with all her heart to get close to somebody, just as I was wanting to slip away, to float alone on the lake.

The young professor had loaned me some books. He had loaned me a book by Nietzche, which I found especially disturbing.

Was it possible, I asked myself, that all things could be so useless and indefinite as Nietzche made them look? I shrugged my shoulders, after a while, remembering the sunlight on my body and on the lake, and the mysteriously suggestive fragrance of the grapes. Such colossal doubt, I thought to myself, was more or less irrelevant to life after all!

I was reading this book one evening on the porch of the main cabin, overlooking the lake, and I was feeling particularly rebellious against its doctrines, when the girl came onto the porch and seated herself in the wicker chair next to mine. Without turning my eyes from the book, I knew she was looking at me, maybe wondering whether to speak. She had looked at me before. She had been down at the camp for about two weeks. I had only been vaguely aware of her presence, since she was not attractive to my unawakened senses and was easily seven or eight years older than I. But I looked old for my age that summer. I was tall and had acquired a small mustache along with my unusually serious and reflective manner.

When the light became too dim for reading, I laid the book across my knees and glanced cautiously at the girl's profile. I was suddenly stabbed with pity. A look of hopelessness had settled over her face. She was not looking at the sunset or the lake or anything visible from the cabin porch, but her eyes were wide open.

She is a little stenographer from Saint Louis or Kansas City who has come down here to meet some young people and have a good time, maybe fall in love and get married at last, and she has found only two young men, myself and the goggle-eyed professor who hates the sight of a skirt, and here I sit reading Nietzche and considering the abstract problems of life and wishing only to be left by myself. . . .

It was only a minute or two since I had laid down my book, but I had considered the girl since then with such intentness, and such a feeling of peculiar clairvoyance, that it seemed to me I had known her already for quite a long time. I started talking to her. I was pleased to see the hopeless look drop away from her face. It became quite animated. She started rocking in the chair, then pulled it closer to mine, and soon we were chattering together like intimate friends.

"There's a dance at Branson tonight," the girl suddenly remarked. "Would you like to take me?"

Surely if I had thought twice, I would have refused. Before I went to college my legs behaved like stilts whenever I started to dance and I hadn't the faintest notion of how to move myself around to music.

But my head was light from reading too much and the girl's manner was peculiarly importunate. Before I knew it I had accepted the suggestion and we had started to Branson. This little hill town was the location of a popular summer resort; it was a mile or two down the lake from our camp. We walked over, along by the lake and hills, and all the way we talked with a strange excitement. Maybe I had been terribly lonely, too, without knowing it, and had only wanted someone to break the ice. Anyway, in the twilight along by the lake, the girl no longer seemed rather too old for me, or too heavy. I noticed something Gypsy-like in her appearance, something wise and significant in her dark eyes and large, aquiline nose and full, over-red lips. I noticed the deep swell of her breasts, and when she walked a little ahead, the swaying strength of her hips. I had a dizzy feeling of wanting to get close against her and be enveloped in that warmth that she seemed to possess.

"Do you like wine?" she asked me as we started across the bridge.

I admitted that I had never tried it. The summer before, when my grandfather took me to Europe, I had drunk some *crème de menthe* as soon as the bar opened, a few miles out at sea, and had become violently seasick immediately afterwards. I had disliked the smell of alcohol ever since.

"But this will be different." she said. "Do you smell those grapes?"

We paused in the middle of the bridge, and sure enough, the wind from down the lake carried to us the grapes' elusive fragrances.

"It's delicious!" I cried.

"I know a place, an old hillbilly's cabin near the town, where we can stop and get some swell grape wine," she went on, "and it will make us feel like dancing our feet off!"

Laughing, she caught hold of my arm and we started running along the road. Her black hair blew back from her face and in her running figure, throat arched and deep bosom swaying, there was something excitingly pagan.

"You are beautiful," I heard myself saying in a husky voice. "You're like an ancient goddess, or a nymph, or a . . ."

She squeezed my arm. "You're funny!" she said.

The hillbilly's cabin was a little frame house on the road to town. In the yard, a white goat was munching the grass. An old woman sat on the wooden steps with her hands folded in her lap. She got up slowly as we approached. Wordlessly, she held the door open and we

13

slipped in. These were the days before repeal. I felt quite adventurous, sitting down at the rickety old table, with its worn checkered oilcloth and kerosene lamp, while the old man in overalls and the witch-like old woman pulled bottles out of a hidden barrel, opened them with a loud, popping sound, and poured the sparkling purple stuff into cold tin cups for us to drink.

At first it seemed rather bitter. But there was not the alcoholic taste that I had feared. So I ordered a second cup, and a third. The girl across from me drank slowly. She kept glancing at me in a calculating way, as though she were trying to surmise my age or other potential-ities, as she had looked at me on the porch and several times before that, but I found myself no longer annoyed by that look. It pleased me, in fact, more than a little. Here was I, drinking wine with what was obviously a woman of the world, a Gypsy-like girl no longer very young, with a look of strange wisdom in the back of her eyes.

Who knows what may happen tonight? The possibilities began to frighten me a little.

I leaned far back in my chair, tilting against the stovepipe, and returned her smile in a manner that was supposed to be replete with sophisticated suggestion. We looked at each other for some time that way, as though with an understanding too deep for words. Slowly the girl lifted her eyebrows, then narrowed her eyes till they were two slits of luminous black. Her heavy, painted lips fell slightly open, and she, too, relaxed in her chair, as though a question had been asked and a satisfactory answer been given. It almost seemed that I could hear her purring under her breath, contentedly, like a cat.

"I have been so lonely at the camp," she murmured, "that it hasn't seemed like a real vacation until tonight."

She lifted the cup with both hands, but instead of drinking, she breathed its fragrance deeply. She smiled slightly over the brim of the cup:

"It's sort of bittersweet, isn't it?" she said softly. "It always makes me feel like laughing or crying or something."

When we left the cabin, the white goat in the yard looked to me like a fantastic horned monster. The dusty road rocked under my feet. Everything seemed quite unreasonably amusing. Laughing loudly, I caught the girl's arm, and she, more than returning my pressure, laughed with me, but all the while kept glancing speculatively up at my face.

"Are you sure you aren't too tight to dance?" she asked.

Her voice seemed absurdly serious.

"Too tight!" I screamed. "Why, I've never been so *loose* in all my *life*!"

I was startled by the hysterical sound of my voice, almost like a girl's. I staggered against the dark young woman and she put a sustaining arm around my back. It seemed awfully silly. She was nearly a foot shorter than I, and here she was holding me up.

"Leave me alone," I told her severely. "I can walk all right by myself!"

She laughed a little.

"How old are you?" she asked abruptly.

"Nineteen," I lied.

"Really? I didn't know you were quite so young as that," she said.

For a while afterwards she seemed quieter and more distant. Then we came into Branson. There were clusters of glazed lamps along the street. There were bright drugstores and restaurants and a picture show with a shiny tin portico and gaudy placards. Everywhere there were gay, holiday crowds in white linens and flannels and colorful sweaters. Down by the lake, the band was playing noisily and everyone was flocking in that direction.

Then she seemed to come alive again. She caught my arm.

"I'm crazy to dance!" she said. "It seems like my vacation is just beginning!"

The dance hall was a long log building, open except for screens, and lighted by Japanese lanterns that swayed constantly in the wind. My physical drunkenness left as soon as we stepped on the floor. For the first time I found that I could move myself to music. My feet slid effortlessly along the wax floor and the girl's body was suppliant to mine. It was more than suppliant. I caught her tighter and tighter against me. The warmth of her body surged through my linen suit. Her breath was damp against my throat. Her fingers caught at my shoulder. She seemed to be asking for an even closer embrace than I could give. Then I experienced something that I had never before experienced with a girl. I felt ashamed and tried to loosen my hold. But to my amazement she only clung tighter. She pressed her lips against my throat and clung as though she were drunk, drunker than I had been on the moonlit road. Her feet became tangled with mine, her body drooped, and I seemed to be dragging her along the floor. My warm feeling passed. I looked around at the strange faces surrounding the floor. It seemed that everyone was staring at us. I stopped abruptly at the edge of the floor.

"Let's go out for a while." I said, without looking at her.

She must have misunderstood my averted face, the strained quality of my voice. She repeated the words like an echo, "Let's go out for a while."

We went down the wooden steps from the dance hall and down the wooden walk to the beach.

Here it was all smooth sand, a pale silver in the moonlight, stretching for a mile or two up and down the lake. The wind was blowing with a new coolness that hinted of rain, although the clouds were still scattered.

The girl caught my arm and stopped for a moment at the end of the wooden walk.

"Do you smell the grapes?" she asked.

I shuddered slightly. I had drunk too much of the wine. The intoxication was passing and the taste in my mouth was cloyingly sweet.

"Where are you going?" I called to the girl.

Laughing wildly, she had started running along the sand.

After a while, we both looked around. We discovered that the amusement resort—and even the lights of the town—had disappeared. There was only the moon and the stars and the wide silence of the lake and the sand crunching under our feet. I felt like an inexperienced swimmer who finds himself suddenly beyond his depth. But the girl's face was fairly shining with some inner violence. She fell down on the sand, and pressed her hands against it, and swept them out like a swimmer, again and again. It seemed to me that she was moaning a little, deep in her throat, or purring again like a cat. I was tempted to slip away from her. All my lightness and exuberance were gone. I didn't feel like awaiting the development of that which seemed to be possessing the girl. I was no longer flattered or stirred. She didn't seem to be aware of me, for the moment, but only of something inside of herself, a drunken feeling, that made her rub her hands over the sand in a gesture that seemed to me vaguely obscene.

It may have been that I was fascinated, it may have been that I was frightened or repelled. My emotions were cloaked in a dullness that made them, for a long time afterwards, hard to describe. At any rate, I found it impossible to leave her there. My feet were rooted in the silver sand. I stood above her, breathing the cloying sweetness of grapes on the wind, and waiting for the girl's private ecstasy to pass.

At length, she lifted her head, from where she was stooping low upon the sand, swept her hair back with one hand, and extended toward me the other. Dizzily I fell down beside her and somehow or other we were kissing and her tongue had slid between my lips. All the while, though my actions were those of a male possessed by passion, my mind was standing above her with a dull revulsion. Her Gypsy-like darkness, the heaviness of her form, the black wisdom of her eyes were now laid bare of secrets. I knew why she was lonely, why she said she had been so terribly lonely until tonight. For all my manly aspirations, I couldn't help fearing the girl. Catching at my shoulders, she fell back on the sand. She was breathing heavily and her breath smelled of wine.

"Let's go back to the dance," I muttered.

"No, I'm tired of the dance," she said. "Why do you act so funny? Don't you like me? Am I ugly or something?"

Good God, what is wrong with you? I said to myself. *You know what she wants! You aren't a kid anymore!*

But I couldn't endure the winey sweetness of her breath. I turned my face away and got up from the sand.

"Let's go swimming!" I suggested wildly.

"All right!" she agreed.

Too late I realized that we had no suits for swimming. The girl was already tearing the clothes from her body. She plunged quite naked into the lake. I could only do likewise. Numbly, I removed my clothes and followed her. The cool of the lake broke through the dream-like numbness of my body and mind. I felt chilled and awakened. For a while, my exuberance of the earlier evening returned. We swam and played in the water like children. I didn't think of her nakedness nor of mine. I swam far out and then swam in again. When I climbed out on the sand I was exhausted and lay down and looked at the starry sky, almost forgetting the girl and what had happened between us a few minutes before.

The wind from the lake turned colder. I began to shake uncontrollably. The girl was still splashing and swimming in the water, crying out as though she had gone quite mad. I rose from the beach and started to get my clothes. But then she dashed out of the water.

"You're still wet!" she cried. "Why do you act so funny?"

Weakly, I sank down again on the sand. The girl was laughing at me. She ran over to the willow where she had hung her clothes. She came back with the little white coat that she had carried to the dance.

"Here!" she said. "This will keep us both warm!"

Staring up at this garment that whipped above me like a white ghost in the wind from the lake, observing its length and its breadth and even its thickness, I slowly understood her words, what they meant, what they could only mean. I saw that she was smiling in the moonlight. Her black hair blew away from her face. She stood between me and the wind and I breathed the warmth of her body mingled with the cloying sweetness of the grapes. With a sudden fury, I caught at her white legs. I pulled her down in the sand. The coat was forgotten, and the cold wind and the lake, and I scarcely knew whether I hated or loved.

It rained the next morning, starting quite early, before breakfast, and continuing till noon. I didn't get up. I lay all morning on my bed in the small log cabin, feeling exhausted and rather ill. I looked out at the grey rain and listened to the grey sound of it on the roof. When I finally came out, I found that the Springfield bus had come and gone. The girl's vacation was over and for several hours she had been on her way back to her job in a Kansas City life insurance office. I was relieved.

By noon the rain had dwindled away. The wind rose up again, the clouds were scattered like foam. The grey lake was turning green beneath a blazing sun. But in the rain-freshened air there was already the tonic coolness of the coming fall.

After dinner I stood facing the lake, breathing deep, and suddenly there rushed in upon me the old longing to escape from the camp and the restless gaiety of its population and to be by myself on the lake. I ran back to the cabin and put on my swimming trunks. I took a pair of oars from the manager's office and sprinted down to the rickety wharf. I felt the eyes of the porch loungers following me down, the eyes of new young girls and young men who had arrived at the camp that morning, and I felt proud of myself, proud of my deeply bronzed skin and my well-conditioned body, but most of all, proud of my freedom, my loneliness that asked only to be left alone. It seemed to me that only I and the lake belonged here; I and the lake and the sun. The others were presumptuous intruders. These weekenders, with their pale skins and slow muscles and feverish friendliness, could never belong in this country, could never share in my mystical companionship with the lake and the hills and the sun.

The girl was gone. They would go, too.

Without glancing back, I loosened one of the boats from the wharf and rowed out to the center of the lake. I lay down in the bottom of the boat and surrendered myself to the leisurely tide of dreams.

But there was something wrong. Maybe it was the unusual coolness of the wind, the lightness of the rain-freshened air, the barely perceptible decline of summer. But I was restless. I turned from one side to the other. The hard ridges in the bottom of the boat irritated my skin. The sun wasn't warm enough, the wind was too cool.

Swiftly, the boat moved down between the hills. The rain-swell on creeks had made the current strong that morning. The wind was bearing from up the lake. The boat moved swiftly, easily, as if carried by sails. The hills dwindled, the bare cliffs fell away, the lake widened and widened till finally I found myself in an open country. On either side were the vast fields of *grapes*, *grapes*, *grapes*! And though the boat drifted now in the very center of the wide lake, their odor came toward me stronger and sweeter every moment till it seemed that my mouth was filled with their purple wine and my whole body suffused with their warmth.

I lay in the bottom of the boat, twisting and groaning aloud, crying with the terrible loneliness of the flesh, remembering the lips of the girl against my lips, remembering the warmth of her body, remembering the Gypsy-darkness of her face, the wildness of her hair and eyes, and most of all, the passionate sweetness of her embrace, dark and sweet, almost cloyingly sweet, like the rich, purple fragrance of the grapes.

In a sort of terror, I grasped the oars and started rowing furiously back to the camp. I no longer wanted to be alone. I had never drifted so far as the grape fields, nor breathed their purple haunting sweetness so deeply before. Now I wanted to return to the camp and its people. I wanted to feel them moving closely and warmly around me. I wanted to hear their loud voices and feel the strong pressure of their hands. I wanted to lose myself among them.

EVERY FRIDAY NITE
IS KIDDIES NITE

When the Reverend Houston was seventy, he was retired from the ministry with a pension, paid by the national church organization, that was slightly in excess of the salary he had been receiving for nearly fifty years from his parish at New Babylon, Missouri. There were no strings attached to this pension. He could do with it, and with himself, thereafter, practically anything that pleased his rational fancy. Naturally enough, he quit preaching. He had been preaching for nearly fifty years and he was getting just as tired of it as his congregation was. One Sunday morning during the summer of his seventieth year he shook hands with his successor—a vigorous young man who would attract plenty of spinsters to the Sunday-school faculty— walked calmly out of the church and never returned.

"What will poor old Reverend Houston do with himself now that he can't preach the Gospel anymore?" most of the congregation pityingly wondered. Their anxiety for his future was entirely logical. When a man has been preaching for nearly fifty years or doing anything for nearly fifty years, that thing usually has become the integrating thread of his personality, and without it the whole fabric is likely to unravel and collapse upon itself like a bundle of old, discarded rags.

The old cleric himself was undismayed. There was a mysterious contentment shining upon his face, which seemed to indicate that there can be no darkness where there has once been light.

First of all, he had a talk with his daughter Dora. She was his only child. Dora was married and had three children. His wife, Amanda, had been in God's keeping for more than twenty years, so Dora was really the only person with whom he needed to discuss his future.

He said, "Dora, you know that I'm a very old man. All of my life

I've been a true servant of God, preaching his Gospel in this little Missouri town. . . . And now I've received a divine warning that the time has come for me to prepare myself for the World Beyond. I feel that I can best make these preparations in solitude . . . away from family and friends . . . perhaps in some strange city where new ways will be opened. In short, I've decided to move to Saint Louis!"

Dora was appropriately shocked: But Father, *this*! But Father, *that*!

When the Reverend Houston was young, people said that he looked like the young Nazarene Himself must have looked. His face was beautiful and calm and infinitely tender. Now he looked more, if you will pardon what is only an apparent blasphemy, like the eldest of the Trinity. He really did look, with his spiritual blue eyes, wavy, white hair, kind but dignified manner, like a physical reflection of the Absolute.

He lifted one hand toward Dora in a way that was beseechingly final.

"No more, please, no more! I have heard *His voice!*"

When members of an amazed congregation questioned him about this sudden resolution to depart from New Babylon, at a time in life when even the most inveterate wanderers begin to think nostalgically of home, the Reverend Houston merely cleared his throat and raised his eyes significantly above their heads. Dora did the talking. She was more than willing to divulge her father's secret.

"He has received a call," she whispered piously.

"A call from another parish? But I thought . . ."

"Oh, no!" she gasped. "A call from . . . from *Above*!"

Early in July, on a day when hell itself seemed to be exuding from the streets of New Babylon in the hideous bursting of bombs and crackers, the old clergyman packed up a few of his personal effects, surprisingly few, and departed for the scene of his monastic reclusion. He had kissed Dora and his grandchildren goodbye, of course, but no one else was aware for several days that he had gone, which added much to the mysterious aspect of the hegira and caused everyone who knew him to feel, more keenly than ever before, the strange holiness of the old man's nature.

When the Reverend Houston arrived in Saint Louis his first impression was somewhat disappointing. Saint Louis was about a hundred miles northeast of New Babylon and he naturally thought it would be a little cooler. When he got off the train he found that Saint Louis was just as hot in July as New Babylon was. In fact, he felt a little hotter. Well, he no longer needed to wear this heavy, clerical garb. As soon as he reached his new home, a small furnished apartment in the west end of town, he would change into something cooler and pack the black suit permanently away. That is, he thought a trifle sadly, against the time of his burial.

He asked a few directions, in his polite, Southern way, and took a streetcar going west. As he rode through the lamp-lighted streets and saw all the strange people moving restlessly around with not one familiar face among them, the old man's reflections took a less melancholy turn. Here, in this strange city, he had virtually no social obligations. Undoubtedly, there were sick babies and pregnant wives in Saint Louis, but he was acquainted with neither their street addresses nor their telephone numbers, so nobody could sensibly accuse him of indifference for failing to call. This should have made him feel terribly lonely. Somehow it didn't affect him that way. Perhaps the truth of the matter was that in New Babylon he'd had an overdose.

"Ah, but that's an unworthy thought!" as Dora would say.

His little apartment was nice. It had been inexpensively but neatly furnished. There was a tiny parlor, bedroom, bath, and kitchenette. It looked like it had already been lived in, as though its tenants had just stepped out the minute before he entered.

Well, really, that picture above the sofa . . .

He looked at it a long time, wondering vaguely about its propriety, and in the end he decided to let it hang. It was obviously a work of art. But were ministers expected to appreciate such things? It was a highly colorful lithograph of a young girl sitting quite naked on the top of an equally naked hill. *It might very well be a picture of Mother Eve, painted while Father Adam is out picking berries,* reflected the old man, *and it really does brighten things up.*

With this off his mind, he quickly removed his clerical garments, dropped them in the center of the floor, and hastened into his new bathroom.

"Hmmm, hmmm!" he grunted as if inspecting approvingly the room's appointments, and then filled the tub with lukewarm water.

A cold bath would just make me feel hotter! he thought.

He lay in the water a long time thinking about his new life and making vague but comfortable plans. When he got out, he felt much cooler and even younger somehow. Unconsciously he glanced in the medicine cabinet mirror.

I don't show my age! he reflected. *Why, I could pass for a man of fifty!*

Which was not a vain delusion. The necessary self-discipline of a clerical life had kept him quite youthful. He would probably linger on in this solitary state for a good many years.

Retiring to his bedroom he put on a pair of pyjamas. He had always liked fancy pyjamas and tonight for some reason he put on a pair of his fanciest.

"A clergyman don't get much chance to wear bright colors on the outside, so I make up for it in my pyjamas!" he used to explain when neighbors poked sly fun at the gorgeously-colored nightclothes that made his backyard, on washdays, look something like an Oriental bazaar.

Here in the city, where all the people were so busy about their own business, who would bother to question him about these little worldly eccentricities of his?

"Hmmm, hmmm," he grunted, not unhappily, as he tied the braided cord. The pyjamas were black and gold silk, executed in the Russian manner. Looking in the long mirror on the closed door, he thought that they gave him a rather romantic look. He was seventy, of course, but even at seventy . . .

Suddenly he glanced out the window.

"Good heavens! Forgot to pull the shade down! Ah, well . . ."

He sank contentedly onto the bed and bounced a little to test its springs. It was softer than the bed at home, the bed that he and Amanda . . .

I'm a very lonely man, he reflected promptly.

For a while he remained in the bedroom, soaking himself in its luxurious stillness, as he had in the tub of luke-warm water. There was beauty in this stillness. It was sweeter to his ears, somehow, than sacred music sung by a fine church choir. People had often spoken about the noise and confusion of the city. But he couldn't remember ever having spent an evening in New Babylon as quiet as this. Though Dora's family had their own little cottage, he had always enjoyed considerably more of their companionship than he had felt he had any right to expect. They had lived right across the street from the rectory. Dora had usually prepared their meals in his kitchen. Saved him the expense of a cook. And it was so nice, all of them eating together. Dora was an amateur dietician, by the way, and the meals were closely calculated to supply plenty of roughage for the kiddies without aggravating her husband's tendency toward high-blood pressure. The Reverend Houston's stomach required no special consideration in the kitchen and received none. Even between meals he never suffered from loneliness. The kiddies had converted his attic into a playroom. Dora's husband was also around the place quite a bit. Ralph was a good-hearted fellow. He was a carpenter. Employment was scarce in New Babylon, but he kept in practice. Oh, yes, there were always plenty of little things around home to keep him busy. The rectory was a frame building. There was always somewhere a loose board or a broken shingle.

Sometimes the old Reverend Houston caught himself wishing that either his Saviour or his son-in-law had practiced a different trade, it was so hard to think of them both pounding nails into wood, especially when he was feeling drowsy after an evening meal.

"I'm a very lonely man," he suddenly repeated, vigorously shaking his head. Then he added with a more obvious cheerfulness, "But I still have a belly for supper!"

He had stopped at the corner grocer's to purchase some food supplies. Now he went into his little kitchenette to prepare his first solitary meal. The Reverend Houston took a sheer delight in good food that caused him some conscientious embarrassment when eating in company. It was hard for him to eat decorously as a clergyman should. He would anticipate so keenly each savory morsel, while he was delicately spearing it with his fork and lifting it gracefully to his lips, that the actual consummation of grinding it between his jaws was often a disheartening anticlimax.

Tonight he glanced gratefully around at the kitchen stove, and the icebox, and the sink. Here was the kind of company that he most enjoyed while eating!

He fell upon the sirloin steak like a hungry dog, lifting it to his mouth with his fingers, gnawing every shred of meat from the bone, sucking the marrow, sopping up the gravy with thick crusts of bread and finally licking his fingers.

"Good Heavens!" he suddenly gasped, "I even forgot to say Grace!"

"Hmmm, hmm!" he grunted as he walked sedately into the parlor after his lonely meal. Yes, there it was, the little radio that he had paid the real estate agent to install. He stretched himself leisurely, like a well-fed cat, and walked over to this neatly mysterious little box. He had never owned one at home. His poorer parishioners couldn't afford radios themselves so he had thought it would appear . . .

Ah, well, he thought, *when a man gets as old as I am . . .*

He examined the little box earnestly for several minutes before he quite determined which switches and dials did what. Then he tuned in on a nice musical program and settled himself in the big easy chair. The minutes went by. Time had never passed so quickly, so sweetly, not even when poor Amanda was living. He felt rested. He felt himself sinking into a soporific detachment from life.

"Life . . ." he whispered.

He repeated the word several times and he found his lips curving into a gentle smile.

After a while some comedians came on the air and some of the things they said . . . The Reverend Houston heard himself chuckling deep down in his throat, as he chuckled when New Babylon mothers told him the cute little things that their infants were saying, only to-night his chuckling gave him a curiously more personal satisfaction. He wondered what Dora would think, what she would say, if she could hear him chuckling like this at a couple of comedians!

"Not like you, father!"

"Ah, but there's nothing sinful, my dear, about a little good-natured joking!"

By and by he looked at his watch. It was nearly ten. In a few minutes he would be feeling sleepy, so he had better write that letter to Dora at once. He'd promised her that he would write once a week, beginning his very first evening in Saint Louis. Now that was rather silly of him, wasn't it! What could he possibly write her about once a week?

He went over to the mantel and set the little mahogany clock. He wound it and observed, with satisfaction, pressing it against one ear, that it seemed to be running quite smoothly.

"Everything, everything," he whispered, "is running quite smoothly!"

Then he went into his bedroom. Before he could switch on the light, he noticed the golden twinkling of a theater sign across the street. He left his light off, walked over to the window, perched himself comfortably upon the sill and gazed raptly down. The illuminated letters on one side announced the evening's program.

It's a double-program. Now that is very nice, isn't it!

All during the first picture you could enjoy the comforting knowledge that when it was over you wouldn't have to go home. There would be another picture right afterwards. And after the second picture you would really be sleepy and ready for bed.

Vera Preston in *The Lawless Wife* was one of the pictures. The other was Hugh Silvers in *Dancing Dandies*. Both of these pictures had been on the condemned list at home. At home he would never have dared, but here in Saint Louis where nobody knew him . . .

At home in New Babylon, there had recently been a crusade against the moving-pictures. Some loud-mouthed evangelist from Memphis had started it all. One night, during his series of revival meetings, he had invited all of the local clergymen to occupy seats on his rostrum, and as a climax to that evening's exhortation he had turned to the seated clerics and demanded that all should stand up who pledged their support in fighting the invidious propaganda that the devil was issuing from his earthly citadel at Hollywood. Of course the Reverend Houston had felt obliged to stand up with the others, although personally he could see no harm in the movies. They were, in fact, one of his dearest indulgences. But after this unfortunate revival meeting, his visits to the New Babylon picture-house had been furtive, spoiled by a sense of guilt. Sometimes he would sneak in for a second show on cold winter nights when few people were on the street. He would purchase a ticket with his hat pulled down over his eyes and his coat collar turned up and his knees actually trembling. He always imagined that the girl in the ticket-box was giving him a satirical smile.

"Ah!" he exclaimed, "Ah!" as he suddenly noticed this sign: EVERY FRIDAY NITE IS KIDDIES NITE!

The Reverend Houston knew what that meant. It meant gun-shooting, plenty of gun-shooting, and there was nothing that the peaceable old clergyman relished so thoroughly on the screen as the shooting of guns. The cracking of revolvers, the shrill rat-a-tat-tatting of machine guns gave him more vicarious excitement than romantic spinsters are supposed to derive from scenes of celluloid passion!

In New Babylon, gun-shooting pictures were condemned. They put vicious thoughts in the minds of the young. But here in St. Louis . . .

"Well, when a man gets to be my age . . ."

He uttered these words in a way that was neither very sad nor very resigned.

"When a man gets to be my age . . . ah, well!"

Feeling a little ashamed of himself, but hardly depressed, the Reverend Houston switched on his bedroom light. He opened his suitcase and took out materials for writing. Comfortably yawning, he set himself down at the little table and started writing Dora a decent, fatherly letter that she would be proud to read aloud to all the folks at home.

"My Dear Child," he wrote, "I have spent this evening in peaceful meditation. I am lonely but contented as I could hope for. It is quiet and comfortable here. I feel more deeply than ever before that God is with me. Of course I miss the merry voices of the little ones. I miss all my old friends and most of all my dear daughter and son-in-law. But the will of God is an inscrutable will and I am very sure he has brought me alone to this city for a certain definite purpose, divinely strange and . . ."

His pen hesitated for a moment and once again he felt his lips curving into a satisfied smile.

"Divinely strange and beautiful!"

He underlined the word *beautiful* twice, more for his own benefit than Dora's. Dora could not be expected to understand the *beauty* of God's will as completely as he who had studied it so earnestly for all these fifty years!

With this duty accomplished, the old man pressed the stopper into his bottle of ink and wiped the pen dry. He blotted every inch of the letter, neatly folded it, and slipped it into an envelope, sealed it, and inscribed his new address, perhaps too plainly, across the flap.

His lips were still smiling as he switched off the bedroom light and crawled into the sweet, cool bed.

"Now it is all finished," he whispered softly, "and I can go to sleep!"

IRONWEED

The evening was intolerable to Nathan. Life went on in his house in an outrageously ordinary way. During supper his father ranted as usual about the farm relief program and his mother leaned toward him with watery eyes and solicitous voice because he was returning the next day to the state university. All summer she had been cautioning him against risking his life and limbs in dangerous sport. Now she went on and on with it as though it were an inexhaustible subject.

"I don't want my son to do nothing foolish his first year in the engineer school. Now promise me, Son . . ."

Nathan hunched his shoulders desperately against his mother's tedious voice. There was a time when her solicitude might have been understandable. He might once have found it worthwhile to argue down her anxieties about football, explaining to her that it was good for a man because it developed his stamina and prepared him for the hard games of later life. But this summer, football—and even the engineering college—had seemed increasingly remote from the core of living. Everything that most concerned his parents' lives seemed entirely removed from him. Often their stupidity made him desperate, like being caught in a small but inescapable cage. He wanted to seize a pencil and paper and draw them a simple diagram that would explain to them exactly what life was and what life was not so that they would stop living in such an ugly confusion of petty values. But unfortunately it was impossible to draw a simple picture of life on paper and it was still less possible to describe it intelligibly with words.

Nathan was like a man who is momentarily blinded from gazing up at the sun. Nothing was visible to him outside of one glittering circle. The center of this circle was love and its radius was all of the beauty that emanates from love. Everything else, farm relief programs, football, and even engineering, were lost in the outer darkness.

Nathan was twenty this summer and love was a new discovery. He had formerly conceived of it (rather vaguely) as a little girl in a pink dancing frock who swayed delicately against him when the college band played a waltz, and allowed her lips half-accidentally to brush the underside of his chin as she murmured her adoration of football men. But now he had learned that love was not that, but was a wild, naked-limbed girl in a faded cotton dress who ran beside him across a meadow, laughing and shouting, till suddenly she stumbled over her own racing feet and fell beneath him, then lay there, clutching at his legs, moaning strangely, while he knelt down beside her, worried and bewildered, until he was suddenly taught, by straining arms and long kisses, the naked meaning of her grief.

He had lived all summer within this blinding circle. All of his sophomoric cynicism had been now dispelled. Now he recoiled with horror from certain gross ideas that he had brought home with him from his second year at the state university. A college professor had given him a volume of Nietzche to read. He had read it and wholeheartedly embraced its doctrines. But late one August night, when the moon was full, he had seized this volume and flung it out of his bedroom window, and even forgotten to pick it up the following morning. Hemingway's bleak sun, which had also illuminated his intellectual heavens quite pervasively the year before, had not risen this summer above the bottom of his brass-buckled trunk.

It was a windy night between summer and fall. Nathan enjoyed the sound of the wind shaking the house as though it shared his own impatience with small, confining things. Listening to it, he sat back in his chair and forgot to eat. But soon his mother's voice twisted itself into his consciousness again.

"You ain't been eating right, Son! You been just pecking at your food all summer!"

His father laughed. "Don't worry about him, Mother! He's in love! He's hankerin' after one of them s'rawrity gals up there at the State U! I remember when I was courtin' you, Mom, I didn't eat much neither!"

At this moment, the blue walls of the kitchen hovered unbearably close. The black, smoking stove seemed to lean toward him and its stench of cabbage and rich meat became like a finger thrust against the back of his throat.

"Excuse me," he mumbled. He got up from the table and walked unsteadily to the kitchen door. He heard the scrape of a chair as his mother rose to follow him, and then his father's restraining laughter. He staggered blindly down the back steps. The poisonous yellow light and rich fumes of the kitchen withdrew. Now the windy coolness of the evening, with its soft odors of damp earth and moulded leaves, closed about him. He walked along the edge of the orchard and was comforted by the knowledge that somewhere on the other side of it was Mary Hallahan and that when the morning came he would walk across the orchard to the corn-crib in back of the Hallahan's house, where Mary would be waiting for him with beaded moccasins on her bare feet and only a tattered red sweater hugged tightly with both arms against the thin bosom of the flannelette gown in which she slept.

But when he went to bed that night, his restlessness returned. The sound of his parents' placid breathing in the next room was more than he could bear. He got stealthily out of bed and climbed up to the attic, lighting his way with matches. How quiet and mysterious it was up there with old things, whose very existence he had long since forgotten, suddenly leaping out of their cobwebbed darkness, and their shadows flickering wildly, like batwings, behind them! There was the little sled, the dashing black hobby-horse, the midget table and chair, which he had used as a child. In this moment he seemed for the first, and possibly the last, time to come face to face with his past selves. He seemed almost to stand in the physical presence of the little boy he had been, he seemed to see him moving soundlessly among these things: sitting astride the glossy black horse with brilliant Indian feathers flowing behind him, or seated at the little table banging his silver spoon against his alphabet bowl, or dragging the ridiculously small sled up the long hill back of the house with the somber winter sunset glowing fierily over the violet-shadowed snow.

Here in this dark attic, at this lonely midnight hour, his past and his future selves seemed to meet and salute each other silently, for the first and last time: this, he felt, was an *ave atque vale* between the young man that he was now and the boy and the child that he had been.

And as he thought of this, something like poetry sprang up in Nathan's mind. In an almost religious ecstasy, he flung himself down upon the creaking floor, stretched his arms across it as far as they would reach and started whispering Mary's name over and over, because it seemed to him that it was this new experience of love that really marked the division of his new self from the old.

This is my renaissance, he thought. *First I grew into life and now I will grow into love!* And how small that first growth now seemed, why, it had been hardly a foreshadowing of the second.

"Mary . . . Mary!" he whispered.

Momentarily, the fever inside of him grew more intense. Their physical knowledge of each other was still fresh. They had hardly begun to taste its full delight. And yet their secret meeting tomorrow morning would be the last of the summer.

He repeated Mary's name over and over till suddenly a rat, disturbed by this amorous plaint, jumped from behind an adjacent barrel and ran directly over Nathan's outstretched arms. He sprang to his feet with a sickening shudder. And then he laughed. How absurdly inimical this whole world was to the dignity of lovers.

Hearing the wind once more and wanting to bathe himself in its coolness, be pushed a small, discarded bed against the gable window at one end of the attic. He covered the bed's sagging springs with an old patchwork quilt. Breathing heavily with excitement, as though upon the verge of some passionate consummation, he stripped off his pyjamas, raised the great window as high as it would go, and then stretched his tingling body along the bed. He lay upon his side and stared out of the window. The wind was damp and cool. Now and then, when the moon shone clearer through the mackerel sky, he could see faintly a portion of the Hallahan's house. It appeared beyond the wind-swept orchard like a small white ship rising at intervals from a trough of huge black waves. Whenever it appeared, the sensual flush crept under his skin again. It seemed to bring him closer to Mary, for somewhere within that mysterious white shadow of a house, she was lying on her bed, perhaps staring out of the window toward his house as he was staring out of the window toward hers, and perhaps the same fever was torturing and delighting her nerves that tortured and delighted his, making almost intolerable the slowly withdrawing tide of moon-flecked night that divided them both from the shore of the morning, when they would have their meeting in the corn-crib back of her house and there would be no longer between them the bitter intervention of wind-swept orchard and mackerel sky; when there would be nothing at all dividing them anymore; when the burning, maddening heat of his body would be poured perfectly, completely into hers, like wine into a cup, like the quenching of a bitter thirst, or the healing of a fiery wound.

It was now the early morning. The mists were rolling out of the hills like grey smoke and with the fine drizzle of rain, there was the chill of incipient autumn hanging upon the air. It poured into Nathan's body like an enflaming wine. He was weak and shivering from his sleepless night. Now he gathered strength with each breath of the morning air. He stepped through the dewy grass and stubble with the lightness of a young animal. In the orchard the low-drooping boughs swept his forehead with cool, wet leaves. The richly-burgeoned trees hung above him with an air of peaceful lassitude, like wide-hipped, heavy-bosomed women whose season of passion and fecundity is past. It was still summer but the season was going, going, and with it went Mary, her perfect beauty floating helplessly upon its receding tide.

As he left the orchard and entered the Hallahan's cornfield on the other side of the wire fence, a black crow darted up from a russet tangle of old cornstalks. There was such startling beauty in the harsh cry and sudden flight that Nathan stood still for a moment. A new heat of passion swept through his body and centered ecstatically in his groin. As suddenly as the bird's flight, he made up his mind what to do. He was going to give up his engineering course and all his fine plans for the future. He was going to accept the job offered him in the planing mills so that he could stay here with Mary. They would get married and live together in the planing town and their happiness would be such that it would not matter how much he hated the mills, nor how little his parents would ever forgive him for marrying Hallahan's—the "drunken Irishman's"—daughter! No sacrifice that he could make for Mary, nothing that he could do for her, nor give to her would be too great. Nor even great enough. If he could gather all the loveliness of the vanishing summer and lay it before her, even that would be too small an offering, too pitifully small compared to the offering that she had made to him!

Impulsively, Nathan stooped down to snatch from the field a little sprig of purple flower. Almost unconsciously, he seized upon it as a tiny symbol of all the world's beauty that was not enough for Mary. But as he went on again through the field and suddenly saw Mary standing beside the corn-crib, waiting for him not like a woman but like all of womanhood, his trembling fingers let the sprig of purple ironweed fall.

She wore the beaded moccasins on her feet and was hugging the tattered red sweater against her bosom. But she didn't rush toward him this morning with the usual cry. Instead she held herself firmly back, and thrust a hard fist against his chest as he came importunately toward her. Through the rough cloth of his overalls she could feel the heat of his body and even the pounding of his heart. Her own heart felt an answering tremor to the excitement that she sensed in his. But she was determined to play her part strongly this morning. All night she had lain awake thinking about things that had happened between them and with the morning, certain doubts in her mind had begun to steel themselves with bitterness.

Nathan had never seen her like this before and instantly some of his own exuberance was lost.

"What's the matter with you?" he demanded.

A childish flush spread over her face.

"I didn't sleep very good last night, . . ." she began.

"Neither did I!" Nathan said laughing. "But, listen, Mary . . ."

He started to blurt out the plan that was in his mind: to ask her to go with him at once to the planing town and get married. But somehow the words wouldn't come with her standing coldly away from him like that. He couldn't speak such things without her being in his arms. He stepped closer and caught at her shoulders again. She shoved him angrily away.

"Haven't you forgotten something?" she asked coldly.

"What do you mean?"

"You're leaving this morning, ain't you? You're going away!"

Nathan laughed more easily. This was understandable. She was simply upset because she thought that he was leaving her. He was pleased and flattered, and all at once a boyish impulse entered his mind to tease her a little.

"Sure I'm leaving," he laughed. "What of it?"

The light, mocking tone of his voice struck her speechless.

"Well . . ." she faltered. "I certainly thought . . ."

"Thought what?" He laughed again. His eyes were narrowed. His mouth drawn satirically down at the corners. He was laughing at her. Probably he had been laughing at her all along. She had only been deluding herself.

"Listen!" she hissed, blind with anger. She wanted to cry out against this injustice, this cruelty. But he stood there still smiling in that arrogant way, and she forgot what she had started to tell him. The words were all gone and there was left only the mad impulse to give him pain. With an hysterical cry, she darted back to the door of the crib. She tore off the tattered red sweater and lifted the hem of her gown.

"Nathan!" she called.

His mouth fell open as he came uncertainly toward her. The animal-like wildness of her eyes frightened him a little. But when he had come a little closer he no longer noticed her eyes, but only her body and its flagrant invitation maddened him. He sprang forward. Just as quickly her arm shot out. Her fist caught him in the middle of his body and he doubled over with pain.

"No, you don't," she screamed. "You think I'm just a good thing, don't you? A cheap piece! You take everything and give nothing, don't you? Sure, that's your kind! Never thought to give me nothing, did you! Nothing but soft talk . . . well, you didn't fool me none! You didn't fool me!"

Her voice failed. She leaned against the tottering legs of the crib and sobbed with both hands pressed tight against her face. She heard him breathing heavily. She was frightened. But he said nothing for a whole minute. Then he began to speak slowly as if to himself.

"Give nothing . . . I don't know . . . I never thought . . ."

"No, you never thought!" she sobbed. "That's just it!"

His hand touched her arm lightly. Then slid reluctantly away. She heard the dry shucks crunching beneath his feet. He was leaving. She wanted to cry out and catch him by the shoulders and confess to him that the bitter words she had just spoken, her anger this morning, were only an ugly form that her grief had taken. But the sound of his feet, shuffling off through the stubble of last year's corn, constricted her throat and paralyzed her body. She was unable to speak or to move.

But Nathan went only a little distance away. Then he stooped and seemed to search for something among the stubble. She dropped her hands from her face. For a moment she could not guess what he was doing. But when he had found what he was searching for and had turned toward her, smiling, with the thing clasped mysteriously behind his back, she knew instantly that it was a gift for her! He had hidden it there among the dried stalks, intending to surprise her with it, and now he was walking slowly back to her with it clasped behind him.

"What is it?" she shrieked, running toward him with both her hands held out like a child's. "Oh, Nathan . . ."

She flung her arms around his back to capture the gift. But he wriggled loose. He trotted backwards with his hands still clasped behind him. Now he was laughing loudly, teasing her, and it made her half crazy. She pounced upon him again. He wrestled with her playfully for a moment and then he extended toward her his fist.

"Oh, Nathan," she screamed. "Don't tease me! I'm dying to see it!"

But his fist remained tight shut. She shot out eager fingers to tear it open. She guessed now what the present was. It was something very small and precious. It was a piece of jewelry of some sort. It was a . . .

"A ring!" she screamed. *"I know! It's a ring!"*

Unable to wait any longer for him to get tired of teasing her, she suddenly dug sharp, cat-like nails into his fingers. Drops of blood stood out, oddly glittering, on their hard brown knuckles as the boy's fingers slowly relaxed. Both of them stood stock still for a minute. He had stopped laughing. He had even stopped smiling. He watched her now with eyes that were dark and intensely serious-looking. Slowly she lifted her own eyes from his opened fist and a long, sick moan fell from her lips.

"Ironweed!" she whispered.

Her breast had become so heavy with rage that she couldn't speak another word. And still he stood calmly above her, sucking his scratched fingers and looking as though he were trying not to laugh at her for having been such a fool.

"A ring! I know! It's a ring!" she had cried out. And it hadn't been a ring or anything else of any value. It was just a ridiculous piece of purple weed.

Through the suffocating dam of fury, words began to break loose. She shouted hideous names at him that her drunken father had sometimes shouted at her sick mother. Then she snatched the piece of crumpled weed up from the ground and struck him with it, a stinging blow across the face.

He stood there like a stone, not speaking, not moving. But when she looked into his eyes she thought that he was going to kill her.

With a scream of terror, she dashed away from him and ran toward the house.

He looked after her flying form until it was lost in the mist. Then he raised his bleeding hand slowly to his face where she had struck him with the piece of purple weed. There was still the smell of the stuff on his fingers and the itching burn of it on his cheek. There was even the bitter taste of it on his lips.

THEY GO LIKE A
THISTLE, HE SAID

I went to see Father Dugan about you last night, Maud. He took me into his study and gave me some wine. My voice was all choked up at first. I had meant to tell him everything but couldn't speak a word. He seemed to understand how it was. He is a fine old priest. Have you forgotten him, too? Do you remember how we used to sit in the back pew at Mass holding hands? We sang in the choir together, too. Father Dugan praised your voice last night. "She sang like an angel," he said, "and she looked like one, too. How is the little girl now?" he asked. The wine made me feel warm inside so I could speak. I told him how you and me had broke up. "First it was just one guy once a week," I said. "Then it was this same guy two or three times a week. Then it was two other guys. Then it got to be three or four guys. Then it was five or six guys. Then it was so many guys that I couldn't keep track of them all." It was a different guy for every night of the week and once I saw you jump from the running board of a yellow cab to the running board of a shiny black sedan, and there was a guy in each car grabbing at you with their hands and tearing at you between them like a bone between two dogs, but the guys cussing each other, ready to start up a fight, till the guy in the shiny black sedan pulled you into his car and his chauffeur drove off with the yellow cab chasing behind.

Maud and I grew up together. The house she lived in was just around the corner from our flat. My dad used to repair watches in Maud's dad's jewelry shop. Once a rich lady said my dad ruined her fine Swiss watch. Maud's dad had to pay for it, so he fired my dad. Now my dad is working in another jewelry shop and Maud's dad is dead.

I told Father Dugan that I saw you standing in the hall one morning at fifteen after three. "They were halfway up the steps," I said, "and all I could see was their feet through the top of the door. She was standing on tip-toe for about five minutes and then he lifted her clean off her feet. All I could see was his shiny black shoes with the dudish grey spats."

The way Maud and I got acquainted was funny. Maud was a little girl then with long curls. We both used to ride around the block on our bikes. Maud's bike was a beautiful red bike and mine was a rusty old thing without any brakes. Maud's bike had a searchlight on it and a silver bell and a basket. It made me sore to see her riding around the block on her shiny new bike, ringing the bell all the time, with her nose stuck up in the air and her black curls flying behind her. The searchlight was no good for her since she only rode during the day. Sometimes I used to think how swell it would be to ride around the Fourth Ward at night with the searchlight cutting a straight white ribbon through the dark between the gaslamps, just like a train's, ringing the bell at corners, and stopping by just pushing back on one pedal. One day she rode by our flat while I was out in front fixing the chain on my bike that had come loose again. She was ringing the bell real loud and she rode right by as though I weren't there, so I jumped up real quick and I grabbed the back wheel of her bike, and Maud was upset on the sidewalk. She got up with bloody knees and ran crying home.

It was me that hurt you then, Maud! Sometimes it does me good to remember how I knocked you down on your bike that day and you run home with your little knees smeared with blood!

Then one day, Maud's mother came by in her Buick and stopped to take mother out for a ride 'cause she'd heard that mother'd been sick. She asked would the little boy like to come, too? Mother ran in and washed me up and dragged me out to the car. When I saw Maud sitting there on the backseat of the Buick I sure felt funny. Neither of us spoke for an awful long time. But the ride through the park got tiresome. Maud asked if I knew any ghost stories. We started telling ghost stories and had a good time.

Father Dugan gave me another glass of wine when my voice choked up. He's a fine old priest. He never talks about hell. "I seen her parked out in front of her flat with a guy in a swell yellow roadster," I told him, "with the light turned out for about an hour. I seen her mother who's dying of TB come to the window and knock on the glass. I heard Maud laughing real loud, like she was drunk as a lord. I heard her shouting to her mother, 'Aw for Chrissake, go to bed, go to bed, go to bed!'"

When winter come, there was a lot of snow. I went out in the yard and started building a snowman. Maud come by with her sister Bessie pulling her along on a sled. Maud jumped off the sled and stood watching me make the snowman but Bessie, who was always stuck up, went on by pulling the sled. Maud said, "You're making his head too little."

I said, "Who asked you anything?"

It was you, Maud, that was crazy about me then! You loved me cause I was bigger'n you and rode so fast on a bike!

She pulled on her mittens and helped me pack the soft snow. Just then some boys come along. They was Irish and called me a Polack at school and made fun of my name. My name is Zawadski. My folks was born in Poland and they can't read English. My mother burned up my father's insurance papers once 'cause she thought they was trash. At school the boys called me a Hunky and a greasy Polack. I was scared of them boys. When they come up calling me names, I run into the house. But Ma, she met me at the door and says, "You no come hiding in here when boys call you names. You go back out and you fight those boys. You chase them away."

I come back out. One of the boys grabs my sweater cap and throws it in the gutter. Maud calls him a nasty little snot and picks up my cap and says, "Come on, Paul. We'll go over to my house and draw pictures."

I am everything that you said I was, Maud. I ain't a great artist and guess I never will be. I'm just a poor sap like so many others. "The world is full of guys like you," you said, "who'll never amount to two

41

pins!" I agree with all that you said, Maud dear. But still I remember that you once were mine. I remember how it was you, Maud, that told me when we was kids that I'd be a real artist some day.

They've torn down Maud's old house now and built up a filling station on the corner where it was. It was a big dark house and always sort of cold in winter. But we built a fire in the hall grate that day. We sat on the floor in front of the fire and drew pictures. We told ghost stories and drew pictures of the ghosts. Maud said that I drew much better than her. But I was too slow. She was more interested in the story than the pictures. The fire crackled, the logs snapped. Maud's mother came in with some wine and some leftover Christmas cakes. The wine made us feel good and warm inside. We sat together on the little bench built into the stair and Maud put her head on my lap.

"Your corduroy pants're rough," she said.

I twisted her long curls through my fingers. Maud's mother came in again and said, "Maud! It'll take me a week to get them knots out of your hair!"

But Maud just wiggled her head on my lap and said, "Let him do it, Ma. It feels so good."

Have you forgotten, Maud, how we fell in love so early and stayed in love so long? I watch your eyes as you go down the steps at night and wait for them to glance up at my window, if only to show that you remembered my window was there. But you never glance up. You seem to've forgotten, Maud, that I'm living over here across the street in a flat that is just like yours. I keep my light out at night so I can see you better and you can't see me, sitting here by myself and spying on you night after night like this. But I wish you'd glance up just once, for only one second, to show that you still remembered how we used to be such good friends. I guess the fur-lined coat has took you away from all that, the fur-lined coat and all the new men in their shiny new cars! Oh, Maud!

Maud and I went through school together. We were the same age and always in the same class. After school, we'd come home and draw pictures. Sometimes we drew pictures of each other. Maud said, "Your nose is nice, but you got big lips. I guess that's because you're a Pole."

I said, "You've got a pretty face, Maud, but your body's just skin and bones."

Maud jerked up her dress. "Look at that! Is that skin and bones?"

She giggled and pulled her skirt down again when I blushed. I was shocked to see Maud so unashamed about showing her body like that. I had no sisters. I'd never seen a girl's body before.

When we grew older I used to stay on at Maud's after her mother had gone up to bed. We used to sit on the little bench built in the stair. Somehow or other it was always a little different after Maud's mother had gone up to bed. The house would seem very big and quiet. It was almost hard to talk sometimes. Maud's sister Bessie had started having dates, too. Maud would scare me, telling of all the murders that had been committed at midnight in the house. "Mrs. Morgan was found at the bottom of the stair," she would say, "with a dagger stuck clean through her throat. Her tongue was blue and her eyes were nearly popped out of her head. Every night at midnight we'd hear her screaming and running up and down the stairs."

I was getting too old to be scared by ghost stories. But just the same, I'd want to sit close to Maud. One night when we was sitting on the little bench, I wanted to touch her shoulder. I put my hand on her shoulder and it was bony but somehow I liked it that way. Her shoulder blades stuck out in back like little wings. I tried to push them in with my hands. I said, "You got a hunchback."

Maud said nothing, but smiled. She put her legs up on the bench and lay down with her head in my lap.

"See?" she said. "I'm getting big in front like Bessie!"

She took my hand and put it over her breast. She was just beginning to fill out a little.

Maud, have you forgotten those nights in the big, dark house on the corner of Cote Brilliante? Have you forgotten how we scared each other with ghost stories and then sat close together on the little stair bench? I remember them, Maud, if you don't!

When Maud's dad fired mine for ruining the rich lady's watch, he told Maud he wanted to see no more of us dirty Polacks around his place. But Maud's mother loved me, she said, just like she would love her own son. She used to let me in the back way after school. Maud

43

and me played in the attic together all that winter. There was an old gramophone up there and a lot of old records.

One afternoon Maud goes into a back room of the attic and puts on the Gypsy costume. When she comes out again she looks gorgeous dressed up like that, with a red ribbon tied round her black hair and a big paper rose in her mouth. She'd been to see Mae Murray that week and we was supposed to be a couple of dancers in a tough French joint. She gives me a rubber dagger and tells me to stab her with it at the end of the dance. She puts "The Sheik of Araby" on the gramophone and starts dancing. I seen when her skirt flies up that she ain't got nothing on underneath. I can't play my part no more. I stand there like a stick. Maybe she knows how I feel. And maybe she don't. She comes up close to me, dancing round me with her eyes half shut and the big paper rose dangling down from her mouth. She starts waving her hips and dancing round and round me. The record comes to the weird, moaning part. She gets down on her knees in front of me. She drops the tambourine and runs her hands up my body and begs for her life.

"I love you, I love you, I love you!" she moans.

I don't know whether she's playacting or not. The rubber dagger falls out of my hand. My heart starts thumping real loud. I drop down on the floor beside her. I tear the paper rose out of her mouth and kiss her lips.

"No, no," she whimpered, "you ain't supposed to do that!"

She rolls over on the floor. My knee gets caught in her red silk skirt and it tore. She rolls over again. The skirt's torn clean off. I can't make her see we ain't acting no more.

"You're supposed to knife me," she whimpered, "you ain't supposed to do that!"

But there wasn't no strength in her arms no more. The gramophone run itself down while we lay on the floor. Maud was crying when she got up. "I never thought you'd treat me like that!" she said.

Maud never had much strength. She had a kind of lung trouble the doctor called pleurosis. First time she told me, I thought she said "Blue Roses." I laughed. "Never heard of 'Blue Roses' before!" I said. But really it wasn't no joke. It sounded sort of wild and sweet like Maud was herself, but it give her pains in her chest sometimes so she couldn't stand up, and whenever she'd get upset or something, her breath went away and she'd gasp like a fish. The name was silly but it kind of suited her though. She was different from all them other young girls, just like a blue rose would be in a garden of red ones. She was real Irish. The prettiest black-haired little girl in the old Kerry Patch. And I had it bad all at once.

Maud's father started dying that spring. For the first time he took an interest in his family. His conscience hurt him. He said that Bessie and Maud were cursed by being his daughters. He tried to keep them locked in at nights. But Bessie was wild as a coot that spring. She climbs down the back porch and goes out with a different guy every night. They park their cars in the alley and wait for her to climb down. One morning the old man catches her sneaking in. He gives her a terrible beating. That night she packs up her things and runs off to Chicago with the guy that takes tickets at the neighborhood show. He comes back without her a few weeks later. The old man doesn't raise no fuss. He is already dead.

When Maud's dad died, the jewelry store had to be sold for debts. All Maud and her mother had left was the big dark house. The Fourth Ward was getting worse all the time. When you walked at night you could hear the whores knocking the windows with dimes. Maud's mother took boarders at first. But she couldn't get the right sort. Nobody wanted to board around there but them kind of women and Mrs. O'Fallon couldn't have them taking the men in their rooms at night with Maud there to see. She kept saying she wanted Maud to go straight and not like Bessie, who went to Chicago. So she sold the old house on the corner of Fourteenth and *Cote Brilliante* and they moved into a little flat that was right across the street from ours.

I remember one time the gang was all in O'Connor's when Spike Dempsey come in and said that he'd had a date with Blue Roses last night.

"It's a cinch that she ain't no lily!" he said.

Everybody was interested. They started asking him questions.

"Say, when she gets heated up," Spike said, "she can't do a thing. She loses her breath. She can't speak a word. She can't move. You can do anything that you like with her then. . . ."

I stepped up in front of Spike. He was a flashy little runt with buck teeth and a bad-smelling breath. But more dough than anyone else in the gang. His dad was the political boss of our ward.

"What do you mean?" I asked him.

"Aw, you wouldn't know if I told you!" he said. "You're too young!"

"It ain't true!" I shouted. "He's lying!"

I busted him right in the mouth and then I walked out. I seen Maud coming down the street. I smiled at her when she come by. She smiled back. I walked with her down the block. We got talking about things. I asked her if she'd had a date with Spike. She got sore.

"I hate him!" she said. "He ain't got no respect for a girl!"

Then I knew that what Spike said was a lie. Me and Maud started dating. We went out steady together. We never had no other close friends. There was just Maud and me.

Young as we was, we never passed a night after that without making love a little. I grew up all of a sudden. I quit playing with the boys. I was growing into a man too quick for my age. My voice was changing. The hair was coming out on my body and on my face. I was moony and restless whenever I wasn't with Maud. We sat on a bench in Carr Park and watched the kids playing there. In the high school art class I drew a picture of Maud, and it was sent in to a contest and took first place. It was printed in the paper with my name and Maud's underneath.

We graduated from high school that spring. Maud went out and got a job. She sold phonograph records in a music shop downtown. She always loved music. 'Specially hot jazz records. But I couldn't find no work. Maud started getting cross when I come over. I was studying art at nights. I joined an unemployed artists' class that met twice a week in the old court-house. I was doing pretty good, I thought. I worked on a mural for the CWA and some of my stuff was shown in the museum once or twice. My mother was saving some money to send me to school in the East. But Maud got sarcastic about my art after she'd started to work. She said I was wasting my time.

"How long do you think I can wait?" she asked me one time.

She was always talking like that about time. Time and money. Them things seemed to prey on her mind. But not me. I never give them a thought. For me there was just two things. Maud and my drawing. I could let other things go.

So things started changing between Maud and me. We'd been going together two years, and now we was both nineteen. Maud was acting funnier all the time. When I came over at nights she would sit in the corner and sulk with her black hair hanging down over her eyes so I couldn't see whether she was really looking at me or not, or what she was thinking, if she really was looking. Sometimes she'd just get up very quiet like and go to her room and me and Mrs. O'Fallon would hear the key turn in the lock, and then the creaking of the bed springs and sometimes a queer, choking sound.

"It's kind of gettin' in her hair," Mrs. O'Fallon told me privately once, "me bein' ailin' so much and you without no steady job! Now if I could've got me a house out West End somewhere and took in respectable boarders, a few old maids an' bachelors like, why things'd be diff'rent, doncha know. You and Maud could get married right off. Well, maybe it'd all work out somehow for the best."

I said, "You're right, Mrs. O'Fallon! This place ain't no good for a girl like Maud, an' if I can just get me some advertisin' work, drawin' some posters or something, why, Maud an' me're gonna get married right away and move out West End! You can come with us an' take in respectable boarders, Mrs. O'Fallon." That's what she'd had her heart set on ever since the old man passed away. She kept talking and talking about taking in some respectable boarders. But now their money was gone. They didn't even have the old house. Mrs. O'Fallon was still hanging on to her hopes, but she was coughing around all the time and gasping for breath. She was getting absent-minded, too, what with her worry and all, that she couldn't remember what she done with the money sometimes that Maud give her for food.

Things went along like that till one night in November when I come over as usual with my crayons and tablets, and I heard her mother and her talking through the front door. I figured that something was up. So I stood there outside for a while without ringing the bell. I could see Mrs. O'Fallon through the lace curtains over the door. She was crying. She cried like a chicken drinking water, jerking her round little head with the wispy grey hair up and down on her long, scraggly neck, not making a sound.

I couldn't see Maud from where I was standing outside. But I could hear her walking up and down the front room of the flat. Up and down, like when you got a tooth aching so bad it won't let you keep still. Up and down. Till all of a sudden she stopped at one end of the room and her fists started beating the wall. "I couldn't help it, now, could I?" she screamed. "That's why he give me the job!"

Mrs. O'Fallon put her hands to her eyes and crouched over like someone was beating her back. "I might've known it, I could've seen it a-coming!" she wailed. "Just like Bessie started!" she said.

"For Chrissake!" said Maud, "That's all any man wants of a girl like me!"

"You and Paul better get married right now." Mrs. O'Fallon moaned.

There was a short silence. Then Maud said in a funny, hoarse voice, "*I* ain't going to marry *Paul!*"

Mrs. O'Fallon started crying real loud, "What in God's name are we gonna do then?"

"You mind your own business," Maud screamed, "and I'll take care of mine!"

I felt like I had a piece of lead inside of my stomach. I was scared stiff. I snuck back down the steps and went back to our flat and lay on the bed and cried all night. I kept thinking about Maud and her boss and what they were doing together.

"Poor little *Blue Roses*," I thought to myself as I lay crying that night in bed, "it wasn't her fault! It was the ornery bastard's that owns the music shop! He took advantage of her being easy that way. He raped her, that's what he done!"

I felt myself changing that night. My blood was boiling. It was making me hard inside where I'd always been soft. Not that I ain't strong. We Polacks're always strong with rich blood. But sometimes I wisht I was stronger. Not so much in a physical way as in a way that would stand up in front of things and make them go this way or that way. But even in school I was always a dreamy sort of kid and willing enough to let things go, and that was what drawn me and Maud together when we was kids, neither of us much liked anyone else, both of us were kind of quiet and liked to draw. But now it seemed like Maud needed something else, something stronger, something to stand up before her and be a kind of power leading her on.

Next morning I walked by the shop and looked in. I saw Maud sorting some records out. She seen me and smiled and said, "Hello, Paul. Why didn't you come over last night?"

I didn't say nothing. Just stood there looking real hard. She looked beautiful. She had on a little black satin dresss that fit her sweet figure real close. She looked like a virgin. A girl no man never touched. It was hard to believe what I heard through the door. But I knew it was true. I knew it was true what Spike Dempsey had said in the poolhall that night. It was true. And still she looked beautiful to me right now. Beautiful, beautiful, and somehow as if a feller could smash her with just one hand.

I didn't know where to begin.

I said, "Where's your boss?"

She glanced around the place. She looked scared. But her boss wasn't there. Then her face tightened up and her eyes turned dark.

"I guess you been talking to mother? Come down here to start something, huh?"

I tried to keep hold of myself. It was hard.

"Get your hat and coat on. You're quittin' this job!"

There was tears in her eyes and her breath started coming real fast.

"So you've got a job? You're gonna take care of us, huh?"

"Get your hat and coat on!"

"I ain't gonna! So what?"

I come up close to the counter behind which she'd moved for protection. My fingers was itching to grab her.

"Maud," I said, "you're starting out like Bessie done. It will go from bad to worse. Come on, now. You and me have got to get married right now!"

"You little no-count bastard! A fine fix I'd be in married to someone like you! What're you doing for a living, I'd like to know, that you can talk about getting married so easy as that!"

"I gotta save you, Maud, 'fore it gets too late!"

She said, "Go on home, Paul! You mind your own business and I'll take care of mine!"

"It don't seem possible," I told Father Dugan, "she could've forgotten all that! I know that she loved me. We was all the world to each other. We never had no other friends, hardly, just her and me. She can't really have forgotten all that, do you think? Why does she treat me like that, Father Dugan?" I asked. I started crying. I laid my head on his desk. He patted my shoulder. "My boy," he asked, "have you got a job?"

I stayed away from Maud's house for two weeks after that. But it was more than I could bear not seeing her. When I went over again, at last she acted like nothing had happened. She looked so pretty and sweet in her little black satin dress when she opened the door that night that I couldn't believe that what I had heard through it had been true.

I said, "Maud, I'm sorry I acted so dirty that day!"

I looked around at the parlor. It had changed since Mrs. O'Fallon had taken to bed with her cough. It had gotten kind of loud and cheap-looking. There was a big plaster kewpie doll setting on the mantel right beside the statue of the Virgin Mary. Over the piano there was a cheap, loud-colored picture of a naked girl kneeling on the globe of the world with her fingers in her hair. It made me think of how Maud and me had started making love the first time, me twisting her curls around my fingers. Suddenly I seen a big dress box on the piano bench with tissue paper sticking out from under the lid. I asked Maud what was in it.

"That's my new coat," she said. "Wanta see it?"

"Yes, put it on, Maud," I said.

She opened the box and lifted out the coat and shook it and patted the black and silver fox collar with her eyes shining like stars.

"Look!" she said.

She spread the coat out and I seen one side of it was all covered with fur.

I said, "Gosh, Maud! You got it turned wrong side out!"

This gave her a laugh.

"You dumbbell!" she shrieked, "It's a fur-lined coat!"

"Fur-lined!" I said. "I never heard the like of that before!"

I lifted one corner of the coat and blew on the fur like I saw Mike Frelich do in his second-hand shop when a lady came in to sell him a coat.

An ugly look came over Maud's face. She snatched the coat away.

"You think it ain't real?" she snapped.

"Who gave it to you?" I asked.

She stiffened up like a cat.

"What right have you to ask questions?"

Mrs. O'Fallon got up out of bed, weak as she was, when she heard me and Maud starting to fight. "Bessie shouldn't have sent her that coat!" she moaned.

"Did Bessie send you that coat?" I asked.

"Sure!" Maud said with a funny smile. "Bessie's doing all right, I guess!"

"You send it back to Bessie! You pack it right up and send it back to Bessie!" I shouted. "I won't have no girl of mine wearing no cheap floozie's coat!"

"Paul, Paul!" screamed Mrs. O'Fallon. "I can't stand nothing more!"

"Mrs. O'Fallon, I'm sorry."

She moaned, "I know it ain't your fault, Paul. We're caught in a trap, a terrible trap, that's all!"

"We'll have to get out some way." I whispered, squeezing her hand.

Maud had put a record on the gramophone and was singing "The Saint Louis Blues" at the top of her voice.

Mrs. O'Fallon covered her eyes with her hands and then her ears. She whispered, "They come from their father, I guess. Both of them, Paul. Oh, I'll die, I'll just die, if Maud turns out like Bessie did!"

Just then the phone rang. Maud snapped off the record real quick and ran to the phone.

"Hello!" she said, "Sure it's me! Surest thing you know! Not a goddamned thing! I got some company right now but if he can take a hint, he won't be staying much longer."

Mrs. O'Fallon took hold of my hand, but I pulled it away from her. I grabbed my hat and coat and slammed the front door behind me.

"We broke up over that coat," I told Father Dugan. "That fur-lined coat. I have a funny feeling about that coat whenever I see her going out in it at night. Once I seen a girl and a fellow get killed in a smash-up. They was swells all right. The young fellow had on a long-tailed evening suit. The girl was wearing a white fur coat. When they pulled her out from under the overturned car with her face all smashed to a pulp, the coat fell open and I seen she was naked underneath. She was naked as the day she was born, except for the white fur coat and the pretty gold slippers. Now whenever I see little Maud go dancing down the front steps at night in her swell new coat I have the feeling her beautiful body's all naked inside of the fur. I can hardly keep from knocking on the glass, like Mrs. O'Fallon, and shouting through the window: 'Maud, Maud . . . !'"

I lay in bed crying all night and thinking of Maud and her boss and what they was doing together. I thought of her down on the floor like it happened the first time we done it together, that time in the attic of the old frame house on the corner of Fourteenth and *Cote Brilliante*, her down on the floor, crying, with the silk skirt torn and the paper rose crushed in my fist. It all came back to me then what Spike Dempsey had said in O'Connor's the time that I called him a liar and knocked out one of his teeth: "It's a cinch that she ain't no lily . . . when she gets heated up she can't do a thing . . . It all came back to me and I wasn't so sure no more that it wasn't the truth. She couldn't take care of herself in a pinch like most other girls.

Father Dugan said, "Paul, it's easy to condemn. When the scribes and the Pharisees brought before Jesus a woman taken in adultery and reminded him of the commandment of Moses that such should be stoned, Jesus wrote on the ground with his finger as though they weren't there." Finally he looked up and said, "He that is without sin among you, let him first cast a stone at her. One by one the men slipped away." Father Dugan poured me a little more wine.

It was a bright November morning when I got up. The wind was whistling between the close walls of the flats. I hated the brightness and the cheerful noise. It all seemed crazily gay, as if me and my feelings didn't matter at all, and there in the space between the two flats where me and Maud used to play, a couple of kids was digging up holes in the dirt. I slammed the window down hard. I stood naked on the cold floor and looked at Maud's picture. It was a charcoal sketch that I'd drawn of her when she'd took part in the parish-house pageant. She was supposed to be Saint Theresa of the Little Flower. She looked like an angel with her little head thrown back and a crucifix hanging between her small breasts. I thought of her now as an angel defiled. I made up my mind what to do. There was only one thing. . . .

I come into the kitchen to get me some coffee before I start out to even things up with the ornery bastard that raped my girl. Mother was bending over the oven when I come in. The kitchen was warm with the smell of coffee and bread. My eyes filled up with tears. I stood there in my mother's kitchen not knowing what to do or to say. Tonight I knew that they'd have me locked up for killing that man.

Mother's eyes are bad. She can see just the shapes of things and the lights and shadows. And so for a while she didn't see me standing there in the door. My mother is big. She weighs more than two hundred pounds. She can't buy dresses to fit, so she wears an old apron most of the time in the flat. The apron is white. So is her hair and her skin. She looks like a big white bear when she's plodding around in the kitchen, talking to herself real soft in Polish or crooning some old Polish song. She tried to walk easy that morning. She walked on her tip-toes to keep from waking me up. But whenever her big bare feet took a step, the boards in the old floor creaked and the stove-lids rattled. My mother was born and raised in Poland on a farm that Napoleon gave to one of her great grandfathers. She don't know much English.

I started to speak, "*Matka* . . ."

She turned toward me, smiling. "*Mio jajak!* He's hungry, I bet! Wants his breakfast!"

She was standing in front of the window. Her bigness was beautiful to look at.

"Just some coffee, Mama. I'm goin' downtown."

She pointed her finger at me, smiling. She stood before me like a beautiful mountain of snow with the sun shining on it. The smell of coffee and warm bread got inside of me and turned me soft. I covered my face with my hands, crying, and fell down on the kitchen chair.

The boards creaked and her warmth approached me sweetly. We Polacks are always warm with rich blood.

Mother said softly in Polish, "What do you cry about now?"

She put her arms around me. She got down on her knees beside my chair like a heavy old woman kneeling in church, and her voice, talking softly in Polish, was just like a prayer: "We send you to art school, no?"

I tried to push her away. Her warmth made me weak and I couldn't stop crying.

"Mama, I think maybe I'll get me a job and go to work."

"Why should you worry yourself about getting a job? We are rich people now. We got five or six houses. Your papa makes money. He's got a good job. So why should *you* get a job? Any halfway smart young feller can work in a factory or drive an old truck! But which of them fellers can draw a good picture like you?"

She squeezed my shoulders against her big bosom. Her bosom was deep. It went deep, deep back and was soft all the way, and there was something about it that couldn't be lost, that never could turn into dust.

"No, no! Your papa and me, we'll send you to art school next year! You will be a great artist! Don't you give it all up for no dirty Irish *kurwa*!"

I shoved her away and sprung up from the chair. "Don't you call her that!" I said. "You got no reason to call her that name!"

I pulled on my cap and went out the back door. In my pocket was the little knife that I used to scrape paint. All the way downtown on the streetcar I run my fingers up and down the blade, wondering if it would be long enough in case he was fat.

When I got off the streetcar I walked slow up the block to the music shop door. There was a customer inside one of them little glass booths. I seen Maud putting him on a record. I seen he was the flirty kind. Maud was laughing at something he said. He was telling her maybe some off-brand joke.

I looked around the place for the boss but there wasn't no other man there. It was a loud, jazzy record they was playing. The jazz-hound snapped his fingers and wagged his tail to the music. He made all kinds of crazy motions with his hands like he thought he was an orchestra leader or something. He smiled down at Maud. She smiled back. He was the kind that she liked, maybe, the loud jazzy kind that could dance!

"Listen to this!" shrieked the jazz-hound. He stood there snapping his fingers and wagging his tail to the music. But Maud didn't look. Neither did I. We stared at each other like we was sick. The fellow got sore. He slammed the booth door shut and come up to the counter.

"Give me something by Duke Ellington!" he ordered.

"Here's something by Paul Zawadzki!" I yelled.

I smacked him right in the puss. The goddamned dude streaked out of the shop like a cat with ten hounds on his tail.

"Get this straight!" I said to Maud leaning over the counter and grabbing her wrist, "You lay offa them guys or you an' me's through!"

She started screaming like she was crazy.

"What right have you got to hit my customers? What're you doing here, anyway? You dirty Polack, get on out of this shop!"

She turned to the record shelves, bawling and covering her face with her hands. I pulled out the paint-scraping knife. I stabbed her in the back with it. She screamed and slumped over behind the counter. It couldn't have gone in deep. There was just the tip of it red when I pulled it out.

I run out of the shop and heard some guy hollering:

"There he goes! He stuck the girl with a knife!"

Somehow I got loose from the guys on the corner. I run into an alley and ducked between some buildings. I run for several blocks. Then I hopped a cab and come home. I lay in bed crying all night, waiting for the cops to come get me. But nobody come. It was a dark morning when I got up. The snow was falling slow and soft. I tore Maud's picture off the wall. I rubbed out the crucifix. I drawn over the face till it looked like the face of a whore.

"Why don't she tell the cops?" I groaned.

I waited all day but nobody come. Then I known she couldn't have told who I was.

I didn't go out of the house for a week. I just sat at the front window and watched for Maud. She couldn't have been hurt much, cause after the first two days she was going in and coming out of their flat across the street just the same as ever.

Then the guys started coming at night.

First it was just one guy about two or three nights every week. Then it was two other guys. Then it got to be four or five or six guys. It got to be so many guys that I couldn't keep track of them all. It was a different guy for every night of the week, and once I seen her jump from the running board of a yellow cab, parked out in front of the flat, to the running-board of a shiny black sedan, and there were guys in each car, grabbing at her, both of them, with their hands and tearing her between them like a bone between two dogs, till finally the guy in the shiny black sedan jerked her into the back seat of his car and his chauffeur drove off with the yellow cab chasing behind.

Maud, I went to see Father Dugan about you last night. He just shook his head. "They go like a thistle," he said, "once they get started wrong."

TILL ONE OR THE OTHER
GITS BACK

She was a woman of the hills, born and bred. Her face was a smooth, pale yellow like rich milk, and her deep-set eyes were flashing blue like the sky seen between the tops of tall cedars. Her face was drawn so sparely that the beauty of it did not come out until you caught it unawares, like a shy, perfect animal, hidden among leaves its own color. Her body was still more thinly chiseled, the breasts standing out like wooden knobs, and the flanks lean and attenuated like the flanks of a running hound. There was something about her, swift and elusive and subtle, that excited and frustrated desire, that was like seawater to the lips of thirsty men. You wanted to lay your hands on her flesh, but when you caught her and held her, there was nothing there but the hardness of sinew and skin and bone. You released her with a feeling of sick impotence. And then, instantly, you caught hold of her again with the water dripping from your lips. She was such a woman.

She stood now at the door of the house looking out, her lean, saturnine face outlined against blue dusk. It was toward winter and dry leaves swept in the door around her and rattled across the bare pine floor. She slammed the door shut and pushed her hands down her lean sides, and looked into nothing for a moment or two.

Then she opened her narrow lips and called, "Git ready, Bill! Long 'bout this time he mought be startin' back!"

Her long fingers fluttered along her cheeks and coiled brown hair in a manner that was anomalously feminine.

"Bring down your gun," she yelled more sharply. "I'll fetch them lanterns frum the barn."

The man came lumbering heavily down the stairs. He wore high boots. His big form moved woodenly and the butt of his double-barrelled gun trailed along the steps with a clanking that made the woman stiffen.

"Cain't you tote thet gun?" she hissed.

The man's eyes looked uncommonly large and pale in his narrow brown face and his yellow hair hung over his forehead. With a startled movement he hoisted the gun to his shoulder and then stood waiting as though unable to stir without her command.

"Don't stand there like a stick!" she yelled. "Git moving!"

She stood bristling a moment, then darted toward the rear of the house. The man glanced around him like a frightened animal, as though he were seeking some less perilous means of egress than the dark doorway that the woman had taken. But there was apparently no other way out.

Shortly afterwards, the man and the woman climbed onto the high front seat of an old Ford parked behind the house. The woman carried two lanterns and a can of coal oil. The man carried his gun. They drove a piece down the Missouri State Highway and then they stopped. Before them was that sharp turn in the road that was locally known as Dead Man's Curve.

The woman scrambled immediately out of the car and stood at the side of the road.

"Git the car outer sight!" she commanded. "We ain't got nary a moment ter lose!"

"Aw, hell!" the man growled weakly. "He'll be too all-fired drunk t' see Kingdom Come!"

"Maybe *you* kin take chances!" the woman muttered. She retreated among the brush that grew along the field's edge and groped around till she found an old stump directly above the low embankment. She seated herself upon it, but found it too rough. She got up and spread over it her man's leather jacket, which was much too large for her own slender shoulders. She seated herself again, removed some cartridges from the pocket of her raveled brown sweater and started loading the gun with thoughtless precision.

In a few minutes the man joined her there. He seemed uncertain of what to do with his big, wooden body.

"Set down!" she commanded.

"Good sight frum here?" he asked, setting himself down awkwardly at her feet.

She nodded her head and turned sharply away from him. She stared down the embankment toward the highway and Dead Man's Curve.

"He mought be 'long most any time naow."

The man shifted uneasily on his haunches. "We should've brung two guns."

"Two guns!" the woman sniffed. "What fer? I'll drap him awright!"

They glanced at each other for a second, the woman's lips slightly sneering, the man's trying nervously to smile. He looked away first, and started to draw a pint bottle from the hip of his corduroy breeches.

"Naw you doan'!" the woman snarled quickly.

She snatched the bottle from his hands and flung it into the highway.

"Aw, Mary, . . ." the man complained. It was like the whine of a punished dog.

The man and the woman settled down for their wait. About an hour later the snow started falling in big, soft flakes. The woman never changed her position on the stump, but the man moved closer and leaned his shoulder tentatively against her knee. Instantly the woman's tense figure relaxed. She bent over to kiss him. The man made a gurgling sound in his throat and reached up with long, snake-like fingers. The woman pushed him away.

"I seen you was skeered," she mocked, "when you come a-trailin' thet gun down the sta'r! When a man doan' heft his gun to his shoulder. . . ."

"This 'eres my firs' time fer killin' a man," he answered slowly, "an him . . . my twin brother!"

The woman laughed.

"You ought've thought o' thet firs' time you laid hold of me down in the field. A woman cain't live in one house with two men. Least-wise, it ain't safe!"

"Sometimes," said the man, "I think that you hates Clyde 'cause he loves you a little less'n you loves him."

The woman laughed.

"Doan you try figgerin' me out naow, Billy! Only Gawd kin do that!"

"Gawd or the devil!" he said, embracing her legs with his arm until they hurt. The woman suddenly clasped his shoulders with both hands and bent down to his ear.

"I'd ruther it was you," she whispered, "that kept me warm in bed t'night!"

They waited another hour.

"Must've found 'im a woman up thar," she said bitterly, "but he'll be back before sun-up."

The man's fingers raised up again, like the heads of snakes from a charmer's basket when the music is played. They groped blindly up toward the woman's body.

"Yore fingers're cold!" she muttered without moving.

The man caught hold of her thighs.

"What made you cry when you seen him in town with Jess Turner that time?"

The woman stiffened.

"How come you cry all the way home?" he persisted.

"You tawk too much 'bout things that doan' consarn you!" hissed the woman. "Effen you doan' shet up 'bout Jess I'll brain you, Billy!"

The snow fell heavier and whirled in a keen wind. The woman lifted her reefer from the stump and wrapped it tight around her breasts, but still her teeth chattered.

"That's right, Jess!" she muttered. "Keep him long as you kin this time! Hit'll be another cold night 'fore you see him agin!"

"Git up!" the man suddenly commanded. The woman's shivering and the broken tone of her voice seemed to have given him a new kind of strength. He grasped the woman's elbows and jerked her up from the stump and sucked fiercely at her lips.

"Naow git on back to the house! I'll finish this job!"

The woman glared at him a long time through the blurring snow. Then she reached her hands up to his shoulders and pulled him down for another kiss.

"Git on back an' keep the bed warm till I come!" the man said.

"Thar's more'n one shot in that gun," she said meaningly, "but thar's room fer on'y one man in my house frum naow on."

The woman started slowly down the embankment, clinging from tree to tree, with the black reefer whipping behind her.

At the bottom she spoke aloud once more, and without turning, as though she spoke to herself. "Hit'll be purty cold in that bed . . . till one or the other gits back!"

The man swore under his breath.

For two hours, lying in bed, she strained her ears for the sound of a gun down the road. But the wind blew so fiercely now that she couldn't have heard. Once she crawled out of bed and opened the window, she could see the two lanterns flickering faintly in the middle of the road at Dead Man's Curve. Apparently nothing had happened, time seeming to have struck a snag that night. She slammed the window down hard and got back into bed. With every moment the cold seemed to grow more intense and her body shuddered uncontrollably between the coarse sheets.

A short while later, she heard the door thrown open below. Without pause, the man's heavy footsteps went down the hall and started up the stairs. The footsteps were neither hurried nor slow. There was nothing about them, no individual accent, to distinguish the steps of one from the other. She would have to wait for the returning man's voice to tell her which of the two had come back.

She lay with her eyes tight shut in the lightless room. She was mumbling a sort of formless prayer, and her fingers were clawing the sheets.

Without pause the steps came straight to the bedroom door. The door was pushed open. Then she knew. She knew by the sound of his breath and by the faint odor of alcohol blown into the room's cold air which of the two brothers had come back. She bit her lips hard and waited. Her body seemed to shake the whole bed, and it was difficult to keep her breath from rasping in the aching cold void of her chest.

The steps moved deliberately over to the little table. A match was struck and a second later the lamp flared up.

Opening her eyes slowly, as if from sound sleep, she looked into her husband's alertly staring face.

"Howdy, Clyde," she murmured sleepily. "Yore late."

The man unbuckled his reefer and dropped it to the floor.

"Been waitin' up long?" he said casually. But she saw him stand still for the answer with his head slightly cocked.

She waited a minute for her voice to settle down in her throat, and then she answered. "Naw. I jes' this minute woke up."

The man jerked into motion again, stripping off his flannel shirt and dropping it beside the reefer. Then he seemed to strike another physical hiatus. He leaned toward the woman.

"Didja hear anything a piece down the road?"

"When?"

"Few minutes ago."

She put an irritable note to her voice. "I toleja, Clyde, I jes' naow woke up!"

He turned slowly away from her, scratching his chest.

"Some feller tuck a shot at me down by Dead Man's Curve. A double-barr'l gun! Went crack through the windshield an' missed my head, I reckon, by half'n inch!"

Again the woman met his eyes without perceptibly flinching. The man's eyes dropped first.

"Gawd-a-mighty!" the woman exclaimed at last, as though the full import of this news had just sunk in.

The man grunted, turned over the slop pail, and sat down to remove his boots.

"Two lanterns war a-settin' out thar in the middle o' th' road. T'stop me, I reckon. But I druv right through."

He grunted again, contemptuously. "Them that hunt squirrels best not cock their guns fer a man!"

He tore the rest of his clothes off swiftly and came over to the bed. He sat down on the edge of it for a moment to rub his cold feet.

Before she could seal her lips against it, the question thrust itself out.

"On'y one shot?" she asked.

"Naw, . . ." he answered slowly. "Funny thing. Come to think of it, seem lak I counted . . . two! I heerd the second . . . guess *when*?"

The woman was silent.

"Atter I turned the car inter th' drive!"

He lowered his body toward her and buried his hands in the quilt, one on either side of her roundly outlined form.

"Ain't seen Billy," said the man. "Whar's Billy?"

The woman's eyes blinked ever so slightly.

"He mus' be sleepin' by naow," she muttered. "He mus' be sound asleep!"

They stared at each other for a long time and slowly they both began to smile. A faint flush crept into the woman's face. Her limbs twitched under the coarse sheets and the gaudy patchwork quilt.

"Hit's been cold in this bed," she purred softly, "waitin' fer you to git home!"

STAIR TO THE ROOF
OR, EPISODES FROM THE LIFE OF A CLERK

O blinding hour, O holy, terrible day

—Edna St. Vincent Millay

It made an oddly fluid, splattering sound as it struck the concrete. One limb, amputated by the cornice, slid several feet along the walk. It splashed the black skirts of a candy vendor. She screamed and fainted. Two nuns who had been standing on the street-corner waiting for a bus and had narrowly escaped being hit by the body, leaned feebly against a mailbox and mumbled prayers. Traffic was snagged on Washington Avenue, wholesale artery of the Middle West, with a hideous screeching of brakes and bellowing of horns as the morbidly curious halted their cars in the middle of the street and sprang out to obtain a better view of what had happened. People were running in both directions, those that wanted to look and those that didn't. Some were running like headless chickens, back and forth, both wanting to look and wanting not to look, unable to follow completely either impulse. Windows were raised up and down the adjacent buildings and heads poked curiously out. A close circle of spectators formed around the crushed body and edged slowly back as the pool of blood widened. The traffic cop recovered his voice.

"Stand back there! This ain't nothing to stare at!"

Nobody paid any attention. The circle became clamorous with questions and speculations.

"What happened?"

"Somebody just done a Steve Brodie off the Continental roof!"

* * *

Atlantic Shoemakers is the smallest branch of the great Continental Shoe Company, which is said to be the largest shoe company in the world. The Atlantic branch occupies the top story of the company's huge building. From there it is only a short flight of steps to that humming and grinding and jolting chamber that contains the mechanism controlling the freight elevators. From this chamber a narrow door opens out upon the flat, tarry surface of the roof.

It is rather splendid up there on sunny mornings. The sun-lit smoke that swathes Washington Avenue, is like those aureate mists that envelop the walls and turrets of fabulous cities out of ancient times. When the air is relatively clear you can obtain a glimpse of Eads Bridge, scattered fragments of sparkling brown river, even a hazy suggestion of corn-bright Illinois bluffs. All up and down the long avenue you can see thousands of windows flashing in the sun and hear, distantly beneath you, strident rumbling of traffic and dull throbbing of workers' machines. It is essential, however, to keep your eyes from falling a few inches below the eastern horizon, if you wish to avoid the less inspiring elements of the view. If you allowed your eyes to drop those few inches, you would be gazing directly into the windows of the American Shirt Company, which occupies the top story of the adjacent building. Irresistibly your eyes would be caught by the fearful symmetry of long rows of white-waisted women stooped over black machines, sewing invariable white buttons on almost invariable shirts, in a room as hideously barren as a convict's cell. But there is no longer any danger of any eyes intruding upon the privacy of the American Shirt Company's top floor from the roof of the Continental Shoe Company. That roof is no longer accessible. Lately an iron grating with impregnable locks and chains has been installed to cut off the stair to the roof. Nobody but the janitors and electrical mechanics can ever climb up those steps again. It is probably an unnecessary precaution. There was only one Edward Schiller in the great Continental, with its thousands and thousands of employees, and even if there was no iron grating with bolts and chains to bar the stair to the roof, he would never climb it again.

Two or three times every day during the milder seasons Edward Schiller used to climb secretly up the short flight of steps to the roof. There he smoked a hasty cigarette, filled his lungs between puffs with the relative freshness of the upper air and enjoyed a brief illusion of escape. He loved to look out over the eastern horizon with its hazy intimation of lands stretching beyond the river and the city and perhaps continuing in beautiful, clean undulations until it reached the ocean. In the summer you could see upon the opposite bluffs of the river a sort of golden smoke and greenish flame, which reason, rather than vision, told you were fields of various grains and corn. There was also a white thread winding among the glittering undulations that could be rationally explained as a highway that carried adventurous spirits into the north and the south. Then there was the river itself which seemed to laugh at the static city and the static humanity that it fostered by setting an impossible example of constant furious motion, of freedom that nothing could challenge as it surged from one end of the land to another. Over it arched a great bridge, across which long trains thundered, sending up plumes of white steam and black plumes of smoke, which was mankind's peculiar symbol of flight. It was incomplete flight, necessarily bounded by the invisible bonds that chained even those who boarded trains to a certain fixed destination or a certain eventual return. Edward Schiller had never boarded a train. He had never been outside the city of Saint Louis. For the past five years he had traveled with only slight excursions between two points, the Continental Shoe Company and his mother's boarding house in the center of town. His was not an adventurous spirit. It sometimes made him dizzy to even contemplate the wide stretches of land beyond the city's limits. It delighted him to contemplate them from the security of the rooftop, but it stirred in him a sort of terror, and he would often creep back down the stair to the roof, after such a contemplation, with the feeling of a small, hunted animal creeping back into the shelter of its hole. There was one thing about the Continental Shoe Company: it offered its employees an almost exactly predictable future of uneventful peace.

Schiller was born into the dullest of social stratas. He had always been closely confined, always been wanting to get out somehow, and always lacked the moral or physical courage to manage it. His mother was a beefy boarding-house keeper who never let him out the door without a warning to return home right after school or to remain within hailing distance of the house. The slightest infraction of her rules was an occasion for a hard whipping, which she administered herself. Schiller's father was practically a nonentity. Mrs. Schiller described him to everyone as a terrible disappointment. No one quite knew what she could have expected from such a man to cause her such disappointment; he was not the sort of which one could expect anything in particular. He was a sallow, defeated specimen who some obscure malady had confined to the house as long as anyone could remember, and who sat always in a wicker chair, on the front porch in summer, in the parlor in winter, reading a newspaper or scribbling things on manilla paper, which nobody but himself could decipher. Eddie felt only a vague pity for his miserable father. He felt for his mother a bitter hatred. But she had beaten into him such a sense of filial obligation that he could never get loose from it. It chained him forever to that square brick house on Maple Street and to the kind of life that the woman willed him to live. He realized dimly that he was his father's son. A backboneless creature. A human barnacle.

One summer morning when Edward Schiller was a boy of ten, he awoke with a feeling of imminent adventure. He stretched his arms and looked out at the green and gold world beyond his bedroom window, put on his clothes, listened intently for a moment, assured himself that his mother was in the kitchen, opened the bottom drawer of her bureau and took fifty cents from her pocketbook. He walked out of the house that morning with the intention of never returning. He intended to walk and walk until he was quite beyond the city, even if this excursion took him into foreign lands whose languages he could neither speak nor understand. Actually he never got beyond the city limits. There were many more streets to be crossed and corners to be turned than he had dreamed of. But crossing these streets and turning these corners, on and on as far as he pleased, was a glorious thing. It was freedom, a thing that he had never experienced before.

During the day he simply wandered around looking at things. There was a great deal to see. At night he slept in the park. When the fifty cents was exhausted on food, he earned a little more washing windows and scrubbing steps. But even when he was forced to go hungry, he continued to enjoy himself. Every hardship and physical pang of this adventure was more than compensated by the fact of his being away from the dark grey house and the mother's prying eyes, harsh voice, and incalculable temper.

On the morning of the fifth day, he awoke to find himself lying in the shadow of a blue giant. A policeman seized him by the arm, shook him violently, and started asking him a lot of questions which the boy was too confused and frightened to evade. When the mother saw the policeman leading him up the walk she flew out of the door and burst into tears.

"Oh, my God, he is just like his father," she moaned. "He never gives me nothing but trouble from the day he was born!"

"He deserves a good licking," said the sympathetic officer.

"I'm too heartbroken to cope with the little devil myself," she moaned. "I wonder if you'd be kind enough to whip him for me?"

Together they dragged the screaming, kicking boy back into the kitchen. There the woman held him while the officer beat him with a leather strap.

"That's it! Lay it on good!" the woman applauded.

When the whipping was finished and Schiller had fled upstairs, the mother gave the officer a glass of lemonade and a slice of cake for his pains.

"Anytime he gives you more trouble just let me know," said the officer, becoming quite genial. "I'll be glad to fix the little devil for you!"

This was a promise that Edward Schiller's mother never allowed the boy to forget.

Maybe if Schiller had completed that flight his life would have gone on from there and achieved some sort of an independent, creative design. But the flight had been interrupted, the young bird being brought so forcibly to earth that it was incapable thereafter of any further attempt against captivity.

Schiller was a dreamy boy in school. He succeeded moderately in only one subject. That was English composition. He had a certain flair for writing. He wrote stories and poems, which his teachers at first complimented by doubting that he had written them himself. But there was an esoteric quality about everything that he wrote, which soon convinced them that he alone could have been the author.

"Edward, you don't write about things as they really are," one of his high-school teachers once complained.

"Yes, Ma'am," he answered solemnly. "I always do."

She shuddered slightly at this firm contradiction, for the story he had just written was virtually a thing of horror. It was the story of a man who was tracked and haunted wherever he went by a ghostly blue figure, a sort of mental shadow, from which he could never escape. The man was an adventurer. He traveled widely. But in every land he found somewhere, sometime, the blue ghost standing before him. At last it drove him to madness and death.

"Such things don't exist!" the teacher insisted. "You should try to write of things that actually happen in life, stories about real men and women. Otherwise your talent will be wasted."

She struck a red minus after the "F" she had placed on the title page of the story and let Schiller go, but with a feeling of wasted argument. The boy's eyes had remained solemnly, inscrutably, fixed on her own, as though he had possessed some secret knowledge incommunicable to her or any other ordinary pedagogue, which refuted all that she could possibly find to say.

At home Schiller also wrote stories and poems. His mother sometimes found them under mattresses or between the pages of books and was always mystified and terribly shocked. She tore them up, as many as she could lay her hands upon, and begged the preacher at her church to pray for her son's soul.

When Schiller graduated from high school his mother thanked God for Mr. Jacobs. Eddie's father had died, the insurance money had dwindled, the country was falling into the grip of a terrible depression, and boarders, consequently, were paying poorly. Mr. Jacobs was her oldest and most reliable boarder. They went to the Methodist Church together on Sunday evenings and sometimes she confided to him her perplexity about her son's future. Eddie wanted to go to the university. He wanted to study literature and science and art. With a dull desperation he wanted to climb above the ordinary design of living. But Eddie's mother had no sympathy with such ambitions. Mr. Jacobs said the boy needed no further education. He was already too dreamy and impractical and his habit of scribbling verse showed an alarming streak of perversity.

"If he knew how to type I could get him a job at my office."

So Mrs. Schiller forced the boy to take a business course. When it was completed she sent him down to the Atlantic Shoemakers, smallest branch of the Continental Shoe Company, with Mr. Jacobs, and there he was given the job of typing factory orders. He remained with the shoe company for five years, until the morning of his death, in fact, receiving a salary of sixty-five dollars a month, and whenever he presented his paycheck to his mother she repeated that gratefully fervent prayer, "Thank God for Mr. Jacobs!"

Among his fellow office workers Schiller was known as a very peculiar young man. There was something about him, nobody knew exactly what, that alienated him from them all. He was a good-looking, well-mannered young man, but he was so quiet and self-effacing that he could make no friends. Some thought he was stuck up. Others thought he was hopelessly dumb. At any rate, he didn't seem to belong in their amiable confederacy. His attitude toward his bondage was different from theirs. They accepted their hopeless imprisonment within the industrial machine as a natural or even comfortable thing. It certainly spared them any anxiety about the future. The next day, the next month, the next season, even the next year was almost exactly predictable. They got a little thinner or a little fatter, a little more stoop-shouldered and pastier looking as time went by at the Continental Shoe Company, but their paychecks were always reassuringly the same. Schiller had the temperament, however, of an artist. He could never reconcile himself peacefully to this form of human bondage. He was surrounded by locked doors to which courage and the spirit of adventure were keys that he had lost long ago. At the end of every avenue of escape there lay, though perhaps visible only to his subconscious mind, the blue shadow that had terrified his boyhood.

He was a rebellious spirit who lacked the courage to rebel. And so he was silent and remote from all the other slaves. Scores of little intrigues had been launched against him, seeking to undermine his position in the office, to get him fired. But oddly enough Schiller was an efficient worker. Never talking, rarely getting up from his seat, except for brief, secret excursions to the roof where he breathed the air of an illusionary freedom, he was very much the type of clerk that the Atlantic Shoemakers branch preferred. The office manager shared the antipathy of the other slaves, but he could find no excuse for discharging this peculiar young man.

Upon entering the employment of the Atlantic Shoemakers, Schiller assumed the job of typing factory orders. That was perhaps the most tedious work that business could offer. The drawers of Schiller's desk were packed with a ruled paper. When a customer's order was received, the pencil copies were handed to Schiller. He inserted a sheet of his ruled paper in his ditto machine, an ordinary typewriter with larger figure keys and a duplicating ribbon. At the top of the page, in spaces provided for those items, he typed the name of the factory at which the order was being placed, the index number of the order, the date, and the number of cases and dozens that the order contained. Then he skipped down a couple of spaces and wrote in the run of sizes. Then the monotony began in earnest. Across and down the sheet, he traveled, for page after page, typing stock numbers and the numbers of pairs or dozens desired of each size and width. The work was changeless and indescribably wearing. In the rush seasons of fall and spring it became nightmarish. The office manager was constantly on Schiller's neck, fearful lest he should fall behind in the typing and delay the furious tide of orders from customer to factory. Schiller's eyes and finger-joints would torture him. The stenographer who sat in front of him was a crank about lights. Electric lights directly overhead gave her a headache, but Schiller couldn't see very well without them. Even on sunless days the overhead light remained off. Schiller's head fairly split from the visual strain. Little electric shocks of pain darted down his back from bending so close to the page. Glittering pinwheels rolled across the black-ruled paper. Black curtains formed at the edges of his vision and threatened constantly to close in and obliterate the whole page. And whenever he stopped for a minute, to rub his eyes and ease his aching shoulders, the office manager strode forward with a curt warning not to waste time: "Get going, Schiller!"

Furtively he glanced at the clock. My God, it seemed like he had been typing for centuries but it was still just ten o'clock! He plunged into his typing again. On and on it went. Waves of dizziness came over him and he was compelled to sit still for a moment struggling against some obscure feeling of internal disintegration. The boss lifted his watchful eyes and saw young Schiller sitting back in his chair. What goes on behind the boss's sharp eyes nobody could tell. Maybe he was mentally accusing Schiller of wasting the company's time which is the unpardonable sin. Maybe he was branding Schiller as an incompetent typist, even planning for his removal. At any rate, he strode heavily up to Schiller's desk.

"Young man, those are 'X List' orders," he reminded him once more, and then added, "They have to be gotten out before lunch!"

"Checked and run?" gasped Schiller.

"Checked and run!" boomed the boss.

Checked and run, typed, checked and run before lunch! became a hideous refrain in Schiller's mind. This meant that he would have to sacrifice the oasis of the lunch hour whose promise had been his only support. He would have to give up his lunch or he could never get the "X Lists" through. The wheels of industry might be slowed up by his own insignificant figure, and then who would hesitate to brush him out of the way? The duplicating machine was a monster with gaping jaws that would devour him, that would crush him between its gelatined rolls if he didn't feed it fast enough with the purple-typed pages! The ticking clock that might have brought his deliverance was now an axe hanging over his head!

Such was the process of typing factory orders and that was what Schiller had been doing for the past five years, five and a half days out of every week, and sometimes a full six, when the fall or spring seasons were at their heaviest. Like all the other office workers, Schiller had become so used to being involved in the company's great organism that he could not conceive of an existence without it. Schiller was almost fanatically faithful to his work. He rarely even spoke to any of his fellow clerks. He never got up from his desk, except two or three times during the day to visit the washroom or make his secret excursions to the roof. Schiller had made many visits to the roof before the morning that the tragedy occurred. He had found it rather splendid up there, especially on bright and windy mornings in the spring or fall. The building rose nearly twenty-five stories above the stones on which the city was built. It was like an arrow poised for flight toward the sun, but perpetually rooted in the immoveable stones. Only the roof, it seemed, ever caught an untainted breath of the upper air.

This particular morning was near the end of September. The weather was bright and yet Schiller was uncomfortably reminded by a faint autumnal chill hanging upon the air that soon cold rains and snows would make the roof inaccessible. Instead of going up there, he would have to retire to the washroom to smoke his cigarettes, listen to the endless talk about sports, rotating with an exactly predictable regularity from one to another as the seasons changed, and endure the malevolently suspicious glances turned upon his silent, almost cringing figure by the other male workers of the office. The washroom was a scenically unfortunate place. To discourage loitering it had been made as unattractive as possible. The hideous symmetry, which seems to animate the soul of all big business was illustrated here to its ultimate degree. One wall was flanked by five white urinals, whose drains were covered with a wire netting to prevent stoppage, the opposite wall supported by five rusty green cabinets. The older men sat in them whether they needed to or not, as their legs had grown weak from disuse. With magnificent lavishness, the company had planted brass spittoons wherever there was a convenient space for them. There was one on the floor of each cabinet, a perfectly huge one under the five white washstands, and another one right by the door. Everywhere you looked there was that hideous suggestion: spit, spit spit! In Middle-Western business houses the brass spittoon is obviously a sort of patriotic symbol, like the Chinese dragon or the French *fleur-de-lis.*

This delightful chamber had its exact duplicate on every floor of the building. These rooms were the only places to which the male employees could retire for their scant moments of rest from clerical labor. Here they blinked their red, watery eyes, dabbled their aching fingers in warm water, stretched their creaking joints, spat their phlegm, ejected their waste matters, and looked at each other with dazed, oddly supplicant smiles while struggling to prod from their habit-deadened brains the halting miracle of speech. The air in the rooms was always nauseous, filled with the odors of fecal matter and stale smoke, the single window opened close upon the mucous-colored walls of the warehouse, and little or no fresh air was admitted.

Standing on the roof that September morning, and looking eastward, Schiller felt that he was offering a last salute to its relative freshness and its lovely illusion of escape. He was quite susceptible to colds and would never dare to climb up to the roof in cold, wet weather. Until the coming of spring he would have to give up these intervals of relief. And so he stayed up there longer than usual that morning, until his cigarette burned the tips of his fingers.

While Schiller remained longer than usual upon the roof, a new and far more dangerous attack than usual was being framed against him in the office below. The office-manager's secretary, and Schiller's most virulent enemy, had been closely examining the books in which Schiller kept a record of sales on the various stock numbers. During this examination he had come upon some fatally damaging documentary evidence. Scribbled across one of the pages in those books were words that had no conceivable relevance to the manufacture or sale of shoes. He opened the drawers of Schiller's desk and rooted through their miscellaneous contents until he came upon the curiously pen-scribbled sheets, which he had seen Schiller stuffing into the drawers at various times in the past. Quickly, with growing excitement, he made a bundle of these sheets and crept back with them to his desk. The words were hard to make out. For some time, the spying secretary studied the words in breathless bewilderment. It slowly dawned upon him that they were of a poetical nature.

"My God," he said to himself, "it's poetry he's been writing! Poetry. . . . "

It took him very little time to convey this damning evidence to the office manager. The result was all that he had hoped. In a few minutes the whole office was conscious of an impending drama. Schiller was going to be fired!

The office manager crumpled the scribbled sheets in one huge fist and bellowed, "Send Schiller to my desk!"

The secretary triumphantly grinned.

"He ain't in the office, Mr. Walland."

"Then go back to the washroom and fetch him out!"

"He ain't in the washroom, neither, Mr. Walland."

"Where the hell *is* he, then?"

Licking his chops, the secretary paused with a sense of drama.

"Mr. Walland . . . He's up on the roof!"

"Up . . . on the roof! My God! What's he doing up *there*!"

"Every once in a while, Mr. Walland, the office gets on his nerves. He is like Greta Garbo. He wants to be *alone*! So he sneaks out the back door and climbs up to the roof!"

The office manager's face turned purplish.

"Well, I think that Schiller deserves a long rest! Send him back to my desk as soon as he descends from the roof. My God, with that little sense, it's a wonder he ain't fallen off before now!"

When he re-entered the office below, Schiller sensed at once some threatening difference in the atmosphere. Had they finally discovered his secret? Had someone seen him creeping up the stair to the roof? Why was everyone glancing at him so slyly over their machines and their books and their files while pretending to be so busily at work? Something was up! As he walked down the aisle toward his desk he met the office manager's eyes. They were fixed squarely upon him. He could walk no further. His bones became water.

"*Schiller*!" the office manager roared.

Mechanically, he continued walking toward the back of the office. He stopped beside the office manager's desk without daring to look down. And yet he must.

The office manager's eyes were spikes thrust into his own.

"Sit down!" he roared like one commanding a stubborn dog to perform tricks.

Numbly Schiller sank into the small, straight-backed chair that squeezed like a parasite against the office manager's great oak desk. This chair was known as the "hot-seat," the same name that was applied to the electrical appliance in prisons that snuffs out the lives of the condemned. It was a suitable analogy, for many a poor clerk's commercial life had ended in this chair. When Walland, the office manager, had praise to give, which was seldom enough to deserve no mention, he always delivered it in private. But when there was admonition or doom to be dealt out, he always summoned the victim back to the "hot-seat" beside his desk, so that all the office workers might enjoy a good show with a moral benefit, like the old-time public executions.

"Mr. Schiller," Walland began, "your work has been fairly satisfactory. But ever since you started working here I have felt that you were not our type of young man. . . ."

While waiting for this initial thrust to work deep into Schiller's quivering flesh, Mr. Walland bit off the end of a cigar and leisurely drew from his pocket a magic-flick lighter.

"Just today," he went on, "my secretary has called to my attention some papers in your record books, which makes it plain that I was correct in my feeling."

Mr. Walland solemnly elevated the papers like a stage magician waving his hat to show there were no rabbits inside.

"How long have you been working for us, Schiller?" the boss began, for the dismissal of an employee was like a piece of art; it must have a coherent form, a beginning and an ending and a climax, like a well-constructed drama, and Walland was an expert in the stagecraft of firing clerks.

"I don't know, sir," Schiller answered quite truthfully. He had actually lost track of the time that he had been working here; it may have been forever for all he knew. Even if his mind at this moment was not paralyzed by fright, he would probably have been unable to give an accurate answer to the question.

The office manager seized upon this simple confession to heighten the intensity of the scene's drama.

"You don't know!" he gasped. "Do you mean you have been so totally unconscious while working here that you haven't even any idea of how long you've been working?"

Schiller hazarded no answer to this. His face and his eyes looked frozen. There had always been something rather boyish about Schiller's face. As a matter of fact, he was really quite young. He was hardly more than twenty-two. But he had always looked younger, in spite of the tired eyes and colorless skin. There was a sensitive softness around the lips and a delicate chiseling of the nose and forehead and chin that had always given him the appearance of having never completely outgrown his childhood. As a girl he might have been beautiful. As a young man he looked quite strange. But now the youth, the softness all drained out of his thin face, had become tragically old in just a few moments. The office manager seemed to be looking no longer into the face of Edward Schiller. He was confronted by an awful mask. The eyes were opened wide and the lips drawn tight together. The nostrils were slightly distended. Against the chalk white of the face, blue veins became distinct at the temples. It was certainly no longer the face of a young man, the face of a young clerk.

"Schiller!" the boss gasped, *"Schiller!"*

The frozen lips began to move, but they were still like the lips of a mask, spitting out words. "I know, I know!" he cried. "You are going to fire me!"

His voice was shrill, almost piping, like the wail of a child.

His face puckered up and suddenly he was crying, with his head laid across his arms and his rather long brown hair spilling down across the office manager's desk. The whole office was suddenly quiet. All that you could hear was the loud, child-like sobbing of the young man who was being fired. Nobody had anticipated such a scene as this. Everyone had disliked this peculiar young man more or less. But somehow,s nobody liked to see him in his present condition. They had always thought of him as an arrogant young creature who had something in his private life that made him feel distinctly superior to themselves. Only for this reason they had disliked him and some of them plotted against him. He was indefinably not of their kind.

Now they felt strange. They were faced with something that was disturbingly different from what they expected. They began to wonder if they had judged the young fellow prisoner falsely. He should have been arrogant. He should have been rude and insulting. That was the kind of scene they had anticipated, nothing like this. They were almost afraid to look at each other now. Our cruelties are usually the last things we ever regret. That is because we cannot, or will not, recognize them as such. But this, the fact of the young man's crying, was something that couldn't be ignored.

Walland himself felt somewhat shaken. He placed his hand on the young man's shoulder.

"Now, listen here . . ." he began.

But Schiller sprang away as from an attack. He leapt up from the chair. His face was distorted with fright and half veiled by the long brown hair.

"I know," he screamed again, "You're going to fire me!"

He was like an hysterical child. There was nothing that could be done. The moments stretched out and became intolerable, while everyone waited and nothing more was said or done. At last Schiller broke away from the office manager's desk. He ran down the aisle and dashed out the door to the freight elevators and the stair. Schiller laughed to himself as he went out the door.

Now I'm free, he thought, *now I'm free!*

He started down the steps. Then he realized he was twenty-five stories above the ground. Well, he couldn't return to the office again. He went back up the steps and rang the bell for the freight elevator.

Of course there will be a few difficulties, he thought, like one reasoning with a frightened child, *but after all nothing can prevent me now from living my own life!*

He thought of himself walking off from the city, walking into the open country, pressing cool leaves against his face and immersing himself in cool green water. He thought of himself sinking deep, deep into the comforting body of the earth.

From below he heard the jangling of the elevator door being thrown open and then shut.

"No," he thought with a rising nervousness, "*there's nothing to keep me here now!*"

But the elevator was slow. The chains rattled slowly up from the basement. At almost every floor it seemed to halt out of sheer perversity. He glanced nervously around him. Was anyone watching?

"*My God, I've forgotten to get my check!*" he suddenly thought. "*Well, I can't go back for it now. I can't face them again!*"

The sound of the rising elevator became slowly louder in his ears. But the air became tremulous with apprehension. His legs started shaking. He caught hold of the stair rail and glanced cautiously down. My God, what a long way it was to the bottom! And what would he do when he got down? If it were only the summer or spring! But it was late September. Soon it would get cold. He would be homeless, without shelter, for he couldn't return to his mother's home. Not now.

"Where on God's green earth . . ." he gasped.

The elevator was now just two floors beneath him and still grinding heavily up; black chariot that would convey him, a free soul, into the world outside. . . .

But suddenly in the shaft, he was faced by an apparition. It was the blue phantom of his boyhood. The ghostly figure stood before him, apparently suspended in the elevator shaft, obscuring the grinding, jolting chains, hovering over him, leaning toward him till its red features became horribly distinct.

"*Whip him!*" he heard the woman's voice.

"*He needs a regular hiding!*" the policeman's voice boomed.

Then the vision achieved a tactile force. He was writhing with pain. He felt a leather strap drawn violently across the bare skin of his legs and buttocks.

"No, no!" he cried out, "I'll never do it again!"

Gasping, nearly screaming aloud, he started to run down the stair. But the way was blocked. The apparition stood before him again, wielding its terrible whip. He couldn't get away from it. He backed against the wall, lifting his hands to his face.

"I won't, I won't, I won't!" he panted like an animal.

"*That's it!*" cried the woman. "*Lay it on good!*"

About to sink helplessly beneath the lash, he suddenly saw the stair to the roof stretching above him. It was unblocked. He rushed toward it as though dashing through flames. Deliriously he clambered up the stone steps, around the short spiral, and past the grinding machinery to the door that opened out upon the roof. The door swung open almost at the touch of his fingertips, as though someone had been waiting for him up there, welcoming the fugitive to the roof and its golden storm of sunlight.

He slammed the door behind him in terror and walked out upon the graveled surface of the roof. The familiar freedom closed around him and he felt himself growing calm. It was not the freedom of the world outside, but of the world above. It was the contemplative freedom. Up here, he could look for miles and miles around him and still be safely standing in one spot.

Momentarily he forgot the blue ghost. He saw that the morning was gloriously bright. He walked toward the front of the roof till he could see the lands beyond the river. There was a sort of greenish and golden flame enveloping the distant bluffs of Illinois. Winding among them was the slender white thread of highway, pointing with mocking persistence northward and southward, toward the unknown stretches of freedom!

My God, how bright the sun was! But it couldn't last. Soon the fall rains would begin and the city would be wrapped in cold fog. Then it would be impossible for him to look out from the roof upon the sparkling brown fragments of river, the splendid black arch of the bridge, the glittering bluffs of Illinois, and the beautiful undulations, the terrible gestures of the land, sweeping away and away.

"I'm afraid!" he cried out.

He began to whimper like a child.

He looked toward the narrow door. It was still there. And now he would like to go back. He had forgotten about everything, standing up there in the sunlight, and now he would like to go back down the stair and safely out of the building. But the door was closed. It was impossible to tell what might be waiting for him on the other side of it. The tall blue figure might be crouching there in the shadowy chamber. The phantom with the whip. . . .

He began to creep cautiously toward the door, looking to the right and the left to be sure that no one was watching. He could not convince himself that the roof was empty save for himself. He had the feeling of someone standing just behind his back. He looked sharply around. There was no one there. But his feet scraping on the gravel startled him. He glanced quickly upward. There seemed to be a cloud closing over the sun.

The door?

No, it was shut!

"I can't get down that way," he whispered, shrinking away from the door. He started walking carefully around the roof. He looked down. There ought to be a fire escape somewhere. But he couldn't find it. And he was afraid to go too near the edge of the roof. He might fall down.

Slowly, desperately, he paced around the roof, pretending not to be afraid.

"I won't!" he whimpered stubbornly.

But the shadow remained up there. It was hovering closer all the time. He had only a few moments left in which to make his escape. The door was still shut. Perhaps he could open it and run down the stair from the roof. But someone was waiting out there. He remembered the way that the door had opened so easily, at the touch of his fingertips. This was just a trap. They had known all the time that he was coming.

"No . . ." he whimpered.

*   *   *

"How far did he fall?"

"He jumped from the roof!"

"My God! Twenty-five stories! Ain't that a record of some sort?"

"Bet he was dead before he hit the walk, but you never can tell!"

"I heard him scream!"

"Any witnesses?"

"Them two sisters nearly got hit!"

"Stand back there, now! This ain't nothing for you ladies. . . ."

"I know him, I know him!"

"Who're you?"

"I work . . . I mean *he worked* in my office!"

"Yeah?"

"Yeah, yeah! That's his suit, all right! Edward Schiller! He just got fired!"

A long white car swung up to the curb and white suited men sprang out. They broke through the crowd and stood helplessly staring at the thing on the walk.

"All right, boys! Get him up!"

Gingerly, they started gathering up as much as they could of the human fragments with their rubber-gloved hands. They placed them on a canvas cot, which they shoved quickly into the long white car and drove off. Already a man had come up with a refuse container, a bag of sawdust, and a street-cleaner's broom. Slowly, methodically, he swept up the remaining litter of flesh and blood. When he was finished, a janitor turned on a hose and washed the sidewalk clean. The crowd broke up. Cars started moving normally along the street. Windows were slammed down. The show was over.

EDITOR'S NOTE

The manuscripts for these stories can be found in the Tennessee Williams Collection of the Harry Ransom Center at the University of Texas, Austin. Williams often tried out several possible titles and made numerous revisions. "Season of Grapes" has "Girl at the Lake" as an alternate title. "Every Friday Nite is Kiddies Nite" was alternately titled "Age of Retirement." "They Go Like a Thistle He Said" was variously titled "Blue Roses," "Me and My Girl," "The Fur-Lined Coat," "Story of an Angel," "Part of a Story," "Romance in the Fourth Ward," and "Maud, Maud, Maud, Maud, Maud." An alternate title for "Stair to the Roof" was "Episodes in the Life of a Clerk." In its title and theme, "Stair to the Roof" resembles the full-length play, *Stairs to the Roof* that was published by New Directions in 2000.

New Directions Paperbooks—a partial listing

Siegfried Lenz, The German Lesson
Alexander Lernet-Holenia, Count Luna
Denise Levertov, Selected Poems
Li Po, Selected Poems
Clarice Lispector, The Hour of the Star
   The Passion According to G. H.
Federico García Lorca, Selected Poems*
Nathaniel Mackey, Splay Anthem
Xavier de Maistre, Voyage Around My Room
Stéphane Mallarmé, Selected Poetry and Prose*
Javier Marías, Your Face Tomorrow (3 volumes)
Adam Mars-Jones, Box Hill
Bernadette Mayer, Midwinter Day
Carson McCullers, The Member of the Wedding
Fernando Melchor, Hurricane Season
Thomas Merton, New Seeds of Contemplation
   The Way of Chuang Tzu
Henri Michaux, A Barbarian in Asia
Dunya Mikhail, The Beekeeper
Henry Miller, The Colossus of Maroussi
   Big Sur & the Oranges of Hieronymus Bosch
Yukio Mishima, Confessions of a Mask
   Death in Midsummer
Eugenio Montale, Selected Poems*
Vladimir Nabokov, Laughter in the Dark
   Nikolai Gogol
Pablo Neruda, The Captain's Verses*
   Love Poems*
Charles Olson, Selected Writings
George Oppen, New Collected Poems
Wilfred Owen, Collected Poems
Hiroko Oyamada, The Hole
José Emilio Pacheco, Battles in the Desert
Michael Palmer, Little Elegies for Sister Satan
Nicanor Parra, Antipoems*
Boris Pasternak, Safe Conduct
Octavio Paz, Poems of Octavio Paz
Victor Pelevin, Omon Ra
Georges Perec, Ellis Island
Alejandra Pizarnik
   Extracting the Stone of Madness
Ezra Pound, The Cantos
   New Selected Poems and Translations
Raymond Queneau, Exercises in Style
Qian Zhongshu, Fortress Besieged
Herbert Read, The Green Child
Kenneth Rexroth, Selected Poems
Keith Ridgway, A Shock

Rainer Maria Rilke
   Poems from the Book of Hours
Arthur Rimbaud, Illuminations*
   A Season in Hell and The Drunken Boat*
Evelio Rosero, The Armies
Fran Ross, Oreo
Joseph Roth, The Emperor's Tomb
Raymond Roussel, Locus Solus
Ihara Saikaku, The Life of an Amorous Woman
Nathalie Sarraute, Tropisms
Jean-Paul Sartre, Nausea
Judith Schalansky, An Inventory of Losses
Delmore Schwartz
   In Dreams Begin Responsibilities
W. G. Sebald, The Emigrants
   The Rings of Saturn
Anne Serre, The Governesses
Patti Smith, Woolgathering
Stevie Smith, Best Poems
   Novel on Yellow Paper
Gary Snyder, Turtle Island
Dag Solstad, Professor Andersen's Night
Muriel Spark, The Driver's Seat
Maria Stepanova, In Memory of Memory
Wislawa Szymborska, How to Start Writing
Antonio Tabucchi, Pereira Maintains
Junichiro Tanizaki, The Maids
Yoko Tawada, The Emissary
   Memoirs of a Polar Bear
Dylan Thomas, A Child's Christmas in Wales
   Collected Poems
Tomas Tranströmer, The Great Enigma
Leonid Tsypkin, Summer in Baden-Baden
Tu Fu, Selected Poems
Paul Valéry, Selected Writings
Enrique Vila-Matas, Bartleby & Co.
Elio Vittorini, Conversations in Sicily
Rosmarie Waldrop, The Nick of Time
Robert Walser, The Assistant
   The Tanners
Eliot Weinberger, An Elemental Thing
   The Ghosts of Birds
Nathanael West, The Day of the Locust
   Miss Lonelyhearts
Tennessee Williams, The Glass Menagerie
   A Streetcar Named Desire
William Carlos Williams, Selected Poems
Louis Zukofsky, "A"

*BILINGUAL EDITION

For a complete listing, request a free catalog from New Directions, 80 8th Avenue, New York, NY 10011
or visit us online at ndbooks.com